BALLET

Victoria Parker

Illustrated by Belinda Evans

Consultant: Alfreda Thorogood FRAD

*Hodder
Children's
Books*

a division of Hodder Headline

02587

For my dancing teacher, Yvonne Novelli, with love and thanks

The author would like to thank:
Carol Grant (Assistant Head of Movement – English National
Opera), Harold King (Artistic Director – City Ballet of London),
Angela O'Brien (Educational Workshop Officer –
City Ballet of London), Caroline Plaisted (editor), and dancers
Julia Lintott, Juliano Shkreli, and Karen Smith.

Text copyright 1998 © Victoria Parker
Illustrations copyright 1998 © Belinda Evans
Published by Hodder Children's Books 1998

Design by Fiona Webb

The right of Victoria Parker and Belinda Evans to be identified as the
author and illustrator of the work has been asserted by them in
accordance with the Copyright, Designs and Patents Act 1988.

10 9 8 7 6 5 4 3 2 1

A catalogue record for this book is available from the British Library.

ISBN: 0 340 71519 7

Hodder Children's Books
a division of Hodder Headline plc
338 Euston Road
London NW1 3BH

Meet the author

Victoria Parker began going to dancing classes at the age of
two-and-a-half. She went on to study ballet, tap, jazz and
drama, among other kinds of stagecraft, performing in
festivals and shows, choreographing amateur productions,
and taking exams which included teaching qualifications.
She continues to teach various types of dance to children
and adults, as well as writing and editing children's books.

# **Introduction**

Watching a ballet is a magical experience. As the lights dim, the excited audience falls quiet in anticipation ... the orchestra begins to weave its musical spell ... and the curtain rises to reveal scenery that suggests another world – a world where anything is possible. A ballet can tell a story – of animals, ghosts, fairies, heroines, and villains. Or a ballet can just suggest feelings or simply explore movement. Whichever, the spectacular combination of light, colour, sound, acting, and physical ability is always breathtaking.

But the perfection you see created on stage comes only after a lot of hard work that goes into putting a ballet together. Each performance requires hundreds of skilled and dedicated people: from dance creators, annotators and teachers, costume and scenery designers, composers and conductors; to the people who dye ballet shoes, knock nails into props, paint backcloths, curl wigs, and sew beads on to costumes; and then finally there are the dancers themselves!

If you're fascinated by ballet – whether you want to do it, teach it, work behind the scenes, or just enjoy watching it – this book will give you all the vital information you need to know.

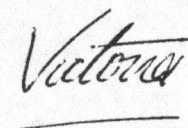

Contents

What's ballet really about?

Ask people who aren't very interested in ballet what they think it's all about, and they usually imagine rows of pretty girls in white floaty dresses and pink tights and ballet shoes drifting dreamily around a stage. But people who are interested in ballet know that there's much more to it than this.

> But I wanted to be a swan.

Ballet isn't always serene, solemn and romantic, telling sad stories about swans and princes (though some of the best-loved ballets are like this, such as *Swan Lake* and *Giselle*). Ballets like *The Firebird* and *Spartacus* are often dynamic and electrifying with fast and exciting physical displays. Other ballets will have you laughing out loud with comic roles, such as the Widow Simone in *La Fille Mal Gardée*, or Bottom in *The Dream*. Then there are the ballets which have little story at all but follow a theme, a feeling or an experience to entertain the audience. For

The Tales of Beatrix Potter

instance, *Les Patineurs* shows a group of people who go skating together; *Elite Syncopations* has a joyful ragtime theme; and *Checkmate* is based on a game of chess. *'Still Life' at the Penguin Café* makes the audience think about the fate of endangered animals and the environment.

Elite Syncopations

Football boots or ballet shoes?

Behind the spectacle of the performances themselves lie years of hard work and struggle. Ballet training is even more physically demanding than football or athletics. Here's what a professional dancer's day might be like:

Monday

9.00	Preparation	Cleaned ballet shoes and chose new pair for tonight's performance. Sewed on the ribbons and darned the toes.
10.30 - 12.00	Class	Compulsory daily class – not to be missed under any circumstances!
12.00 - 12.15	Lunch	Grabbed sandwich before dashing up to wardrobe for a costume fitting.
12.15 - 4.30	Rehearsal	Had to be available all afternoon, but not dancing all the time.
4.30 - 5.30	Light meal	Managed to fit in half-hour massage after eating.
5.30 - 6.30	Dressing	Did hair and make-up for tonight's performance. Put on practise clothes.
6.30 - 7.00	Warm-up	On stage, with all the company. Lots of barrework.
7.00 - 7.30	Dressing	Put on costume and leg-warmers and shawl over the top to wear until my stage call came.
7.30 - 10.30	Performance	
11.00		Home, snack and bed!

This physically demanding schedule can continue six days a week. Some professional dancers may not even get one day off, as they are often on tour and Sundays can be taken up with travelling from place to place.

Not only do dancers stretch their body to its limits, they have to make it look easy at the same time! Imagine asking cricketer Paul Terry or athlete Sally Gunnell to do their stuff without huffing and puffing or showing any other visible signs of effort! (In fact, many sportspeople study ballet in order to improve their balance, strength, flexibility and agility.) Like sportspeople, dancers require not only physical strength but also mental stamina and determination.

SPOTLIGHTS

In the modern ballet Elite Syncopations, *the choreographer Kenneth MacMillan used a tall female dancer to support and lift a smaller male dancer around the stage. Not many athletes (of either sex) would be strong enough to do that, would they?*

But I've got two left feet!

Just as there are many people who like watching Formula One without wanting to be a racing driver, there are also many people who love ballet but who don't want to be dancers. You can get a great deal of enjoyment from ballet just by watching it, reading about it, listening to the music, and – like pop fans – following the lives of your favourite performers.

STAR PROFILE

DARCEY BUSSELL

Darcey Bussell of the UK's Royal Ballet is one of the leading ballerinas in the world today. Born in 1969, she started dancing when she was five. She went to stage school and studied all the performing arts before going to the Royal Ballet School at 13 – two years later than usual – so she had to work hard to catch up. After graduating from the RBS, Darcey joined the Sadler's Wells Royal Ballet (now the Birmingham Royal Ballet). In 1987, she had a ballet, *The Prince of the Pagodas*, created especially for her and from then on her career has gone from strength to strength. She has been acclaimed in many leading roles, dancing all over the world and on television, in films, and as a guest with famous companies.

What goes on behind the scenes?

Ballet is not just about dancing! In fact the dancing is only one part of the staging of a spectacular show with music, costumes, and scenery. Everyone in a ballet company works together to organise everything down to the last detail. Here are the people involved:

The *artistic director* decides which ballets the company is to perform, selects the dancers, and organises the theatres they are going to dance in. She or he commissions the people needed to create a new ballet or stage an old one.

A *choreographer* is the person who makes up new ballets, devising the steps and influencing the creation or choice of music, the costumes, the scenery, and the lighting.

A *choreologist* or *dance notator* records the movements so they are not forgotten.

A *ballet master* or *mistress* schedules and takes rehearsals along with a *répétiteur*.

Company ballet teachers take daily classes for the dancers.

A *scenery designer* creates the stage settings to help bring out the ideas behind each type of ballet, taking into account the actual steps of the dances so that the dancers aren't obstructed as they move. A team of painters, carpenters, and builders construct the scenery.

A *costume designer* thinks up costumes that reflect the characters of the story or complement the feelings and thoughts behind a theme ballet.

A *lighting designer* creates a lighting plan to accompany the dancing on stage. In story ballets, dramatic lighting can create thunder, a spooky wood, or even the sunlight of a bright summer's day. In theme ballets, lighting is even more important in communicating ideas to the audience as the scenery and costumes may be less specific than in story ballets.

Ballet companies usually have their own *orchestras* and *conductors* who are organised by a *musical director*. A *rehearsal pianist* accompanies the dancers for class and initial rehearsals.

A *stage manager* organises all the technical staff in the theatre who are involved in a performance. The *stage crew* are in charge of special effects, the props, and shifting the scenery. *Lighting technicians* make sure all lights work in the right way at the correct time. All technical staff work under the supervision of a *technical director*.

A *publicity department* deals with the important business of advertising the company's work so that sufficient tickets are sold. They produce posters and organise interviews and articles with the media. The publicity department also produces a programme for each ballet which people can buy to find out all about the production they have come to watch.

Many ballet companies now have *education officers* and *workshop leaders* who visit schools and community centres to let people know how a ballet company works.

Finally, there are *office staff* to do general and important administration such as liaising with the theatres the company is going to visit, organising contracts, and making sure everyone gets paid!

Is ballet the same all over the world?

If you watch dancers from various countries, you will notice slight differences in the way they move. This is because ballet training has developed in different ways in each country. For instance, Danish training places importance on jumping, resulting in dancers with a light and bouncy style. American dancers display speed, athleticism and gymnastic qualities. In Russia, the dancers are famous for their passionate and dramatic style.

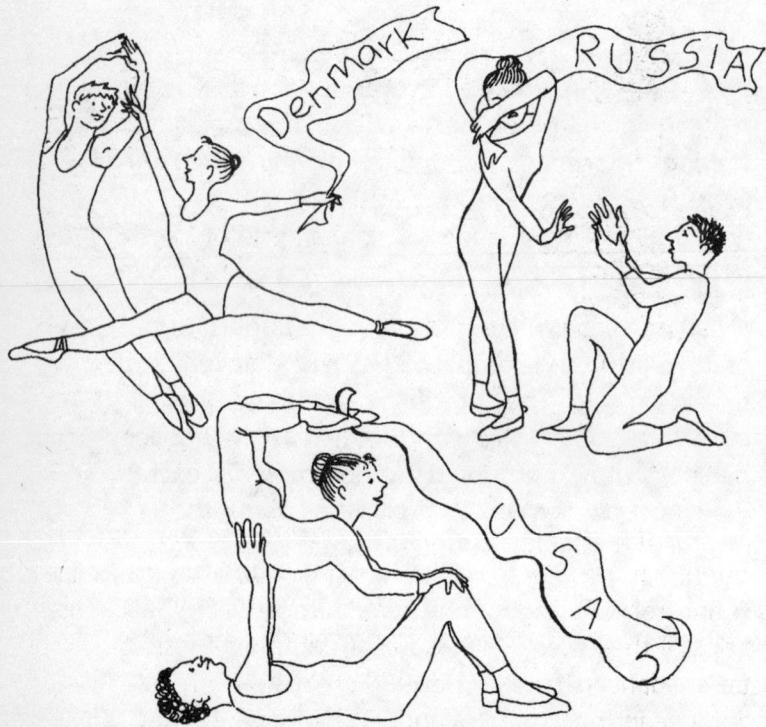

But despite these variations in style, ballet training all over the world focuses on exactly the same things. All ballet dancers learn the same steps and the same basic technique or 'rules' of ballet.

How it all began

Dancing has always come naturally to humans. Since the very earliest times people have danced for all sorts of reasons: in celebration, for religious festivals, to prepare for war, to entertain others – or simply for their own enjoyment.

But if you stop and think about it, you'll realise that ballet is a very unnatural way to dance. Few people have legs that turn out from the top, and no one automatically walks on the tips of their toes! Ballet is full of contradictions. For instance, dancers have to develop great strength and endurance in their muscles and yet look as light and graceful as if they have no muscles at all! Ballet technique is so strict that everyone aims to do the steps in exactly the same way – at the same time as trying to be better than everyone else!

15

So where did the basic ideas about ballet come from?

Ballet is nearly 500 years old! In the 16th and 17th Centuries, European kings and queens built huge palaces and fine gardens to show off their wealth. They filled the palaces with expensive and beautiful possessions and encouraged artists, musicians, actors and poets to produce works for them. For entertainment, they held lavish feasts where specially devised stories were acted out by professionals as well as the nobility. And the more they showed off, the more spectacular these performances became, with performers being given special training by dance masters, and designers creating splendid costumes and scenery.

What did early ballet steps look like?

The dancers in the first ballets were restricted by the formal and elaborate costumes of the time – especially the women, who had to cope with corsets and long heavy skirts. So the aim of the dancing was to parade in intricate patterns over the floor while displaying grace and elegance. The dancers held their backs straight and their heads lifted – not only to look tall and poised, but also to stop their huge wigs and heavy headdresses falling off!

Why are ballet words all in French?

King Louis XIV of France (1643-1715) particularly loved dancing and took part in many ballets himself. In fact, it was his part as the sun in *Le Ballet de la Nuit (The Night Ballet)* which gave him his famous nickname of 'the Sun King'. You can see him in the costume above.

17

In 1661, Louis founded the first school where professional dancers could train, *L'Académie Nationale de la Danse*, and it is thought that Louis' own dancing master, Beauchamp, set down the basis for all ballet steps: the five positions of the feet. These and most other ballet steps are still called by their French names all over the world today.

SPOTLIGHTS

Did you think that, because the international language of ballet is French, the word 'ballet' itself is French? Wrong – it's Italian! (It actually comes from the word 'balli' or 'balletti' which means 'dances'. The Italian aristocracy particularly loved ballet banquets and they passed the fashion on to the rest of Europe.

Has ballet dancing always been liked more by girls than boys?

No! In the very early days men enjoyed dancing at court just as much as women. By the time ballet dancing began to be seen in public in the theatre, all the dancers were men. They used to dance the women's roles wearing masks because it wasn't considered proper for women to be professional performers. In fact trained female dancers weren't allowed to appear in the theatre until 1681.

Have there ever been ballets with speaking in them?

The first ballets were based on classical myths, and they told their stories through poetic speeches and songs. The aim of the dancing was more to show something beautiful to watch than to tell the plot. Even when ballet moved away from the privacy of the courts and into the theatre, it was first seen as part of operas. It was still the singing which told the story.

After a while, the dancing masters began to think it should be possible for dancers to tell a story without using words. In 1717, a dancing master called John Weaver put on a ballet called *The Loves of Mars and Venus* at London's Drury Lane Theatre. It was the first ballet in which the dancers used gestures and facial expression, rather than speech, to convey what they meant. This was when ballet broke away from opera and became an art-form in its own right.

Who was the first ballerina?

Without cumbersome long skirts, men had been able to perform a wider range of steps and leaps for some time before a dancer called Marie Camargo got noticed in the 1720s. Marie was one of the first women to establish herself for her originality and accomplished dancing. She daringly shortened her skirts to above her ankle and performed steps which had previously only been performed by men.

SPOTLIGHTS

The first female dancer to dance on her toes was Amalia Brugnoli who, in the 18th Century, raised herself on her toes in a performance in Vienna. The Italian dancing master and choreographer Filippo Taglioni saw Amalia and went on to develop special foot and leg exercises so that his daughter Marie could support her body-weight on the toes of just one foot - in soft shoes!

20

What is Romantic Ballet?

In the early 19th Century, life across Europe was changed by the Industrial Revolution. People wanted to escape from the smoky cities that sprang up with their dirty factories and noisy machines, and they started to imagine fantasy worlds of magic, dreams and romantic stories. Painting, music, writing, and ballet were all affected by the 'Romantic Movement'.

The first great Romantic Ballet was *La Sylphide*, the sad story of a forest spirit (or sylph) whose beauty bewitches a young man on his wedding day. Filippo Taglioni created it for his daughter Marie in 1832, who enchanted audiences with her ethereal performance.

It was in such Romantic Ballets that the idea of the *corps de ballet* was created as, for the first time, a whole group of girls would dance the same steps together, heightening the pale, ghostly effect.

Ballet for boys

Many people in Western Europe think that ballet is not much of a career for a man and don't encourage boys to dance. This attitude began because of the Romantic Ballets, in which ballerinas grew more and more important and the male dancers were pushed into the background, used mainly in a supportive role to lift the female dancers as if they were flying. Now, the Romantic Ballets have been reworked so that the male dancers have stronger roles. And athletic male dancers such as Joaquin Cortés (a classically-trained dancer who fuses ballet with flamenco), and Patrick Swayze (who only gave up ballet and turned to acting because of an injury), have done much to show that male dancing can be strenuous, skilful and exciting.

What's the difference between Romantic and Classical Ballet?

Many people call all types of ballet 'classical' but the term 'Classical Ballet' means something specific. During the Romantic period, the Russian Tsar spent large amounts of his personal money on forming two Imperial ballet companies and staging ballets. He also set up special ballet schools and invited teachers and choreographers from all over the world to work with Russian dancers.

One of the people the Tsar invited was a Frenchman called Marius Petipa (1819-1910). In his productions, the story, costumes and scenery were often less important than the *divertissements* (dances which don't push along the plot but which are simply enjoyable to watch). Petipa based his ballets around three or four acts, with dazzling solos (for the women and the men) or *pas de deux* (a male/female duet), and grand *corps de ballet* dances and contrasting character dances. Petipa gave his dancers the chance to show off their utmost technical skills – there were lots of athletic leaps, fast turns and difficult lifts. Some of Petipa's Classical Ballet masterpieces are still seen today and include *Swan Lake*, *Sleeping Beauty* and *Don Quixote*.

SPOTLIGHTS

So many famous dancers were Russian, Italian or French it became fashionable for dancers of other nationalities to change their names to something exotic-sounding. Did you know that Peggy Hookham, Alice Marks, Patrick Kay, and Lynn Springbett became Margot Fonteyn, Alicia Markova, Anton Dolin, and Lynn Seymour?

What does 'Ballets Russes' mean?

Despite Petipa's success, another dance-maker called Michel Fokine (1880-1942) felt that ballet should be more than Petipa's dazzling displays of technical brilliance. Reacting against the Classical style, he believed that dancing, acting, music, scenery, costumes, make-up and lighting should all play equal parts in the ballet.

A director who shared Fokine's ideas was Sergei Diaghilev (1872–1929), an artist with a flair for bringing together other geniuses. Between 1909 and 1929 he created a famous company called the Diaghilev Ballet, later to become the *Ballets Russes* (Russian ballet). Fokine's choreography was combined with famous designers such as Picasso, Bakst and Benois, music by master composers such as Chopin and Stravinsky, the teaching of Enrico Cecchetti, and the legendary dancing of Nijinsky, Pavlova, Karsavina and de Valois among others.

Strangely enough, considering its name, the *Ballets Russes* never performed in Russia, but it stunned Europe and America with its new style. In the Company's one-act ballets, male principals were as important as ballerinas. New shapes and movements were introduced which broke away from classical traditions, and the dancers expressed dramatic qualities, as well as technical skills.

STAR PROFILE

ANNA PAVLOVA

Anna Pavlova was born in St Petersburg in 1881. She saw her first ballet, *The Sleeping Beauty*, when she was eight and was captivated by it. At ten, she went to a ballet school and eventually graduated to the Imperial Ballet Company. Pavlova was famous for her ability to transform herself into whatever she was trying to portray and her most famous performance was as *The Dying Swan,* a role Fokine choreographed for her. In 1912, Pavlova married and moved to London in a house with a pond for her pet swans. In 1914 she formed her own ballet company with which she toured for the rest of her life. Anna Pavlova died in 1931.

3 Getting started

Anyone can have fun learning ballet! It's not just for those who want to dance the lead in *Swan Lake*. Some people express themselves by writing stories or drawing pictures, others love the joy of moving and using their bodies through dance.

What's the first step?

Join a class! All dancers – no matter how experienced or brilliant – need to do a practice class every day. The younger you join one the better. A ballet class will:

- Develop your strength and suppleness.
- Give you a good ear for music and rhythm.
- Help you with all other forms of dance.
- Be fun!

BALLET CLASS
Enrol HERE TODAY

Finding a teacher

It's important to find a qualified teacher who can make sure you do the right exercises in the right way. Look in your local paper to find out about a class near you or contact one of the examination boards listed on pages 123–124. To select a good teacher:

- Ask to watch part of a class before you sign up.
- Make sure the class isn't over-crowded.
- Look out for neatly-dressed pupils in ballet uniforms.
- Check the students are well-behaved and listening to their teacher.

What do you need to start off with?

You don't need lots of expensive clothes and equipment to get going. In fact, don't buy anything until you've tried a few classes and are sure you want to carry on. Ask your teacher what to wear at first. Most will suggest:

- A tracksuit or a swimsuit.
- Ankle socks or bare feet.

What type of ballet shoes should I buy?

If you're a girl, you won't need to buy stiffened pointe shoes for standing on your toes until you have worked hard at ballet for several years. Your teacher will tell you when you are ready for pointe shoes (see page 105), and until then you should use soft 'flats' which come in either canvas, leather or satin. Girls usually wear pink shoes and boys usually wear black. (Professional dancers often have their shoes dyed to match their costumes, so if yours are a different colour, it doesn't matter at all.)

Ballet shoes should be close-fitting and they come with a drawstring which ties at the front of the shoe to help you adjust the fit over the top of your foot. (Make sure you tuck the ends of the drawstring neatly into your shoe.)

Each pair doesn't come in a right and a left – they mould to your feet as you wear them. So decide which one is going to be which and mark them clearly inside so you don't get them muddled up.

Buy your shoes at a specialist dance shop (look for one in your telephone directory) where staff are trained to fit shoes properly.

SPOTLIGHTS

You could ask your teacher if they have any second-hand shoes to fit you. As young people often grow out of ballet shoes very quickly, teachers often have a supply of hardly-worn shoes that will not take half as much of your pocket money as buying brand new shoes.

How do you stop ballet shoes from falling off?

To keep your ballet shoes on when you dance, you need to attach either a loop of elastic (boys or girls) or ribbons (girls only) – although some professionals use both elastic and ribbons. For elastic, measure it over the instep of your foot and allow an extra 4 cm, then cut two pieces like this. For ribbons, you can use either nylon or satin ribbon which is about 1 cm wide, and you will need two 50 cm lengths for each shoe. To sew on your elastic or ribbon:

• Fold over the heel of your shoe, flattening it along the inner sole. The crease that is made along both sides marks where the ribbon or elastic should be sewn.
• Don't sew straight up, angle the ribbon or elastic forward slightly towards the toe.
• Sew about 2 cm of the elastic or ribbon into the shoe itself to hold the heel firmly.
• Don't sew through the drawstring or it won't work properly!

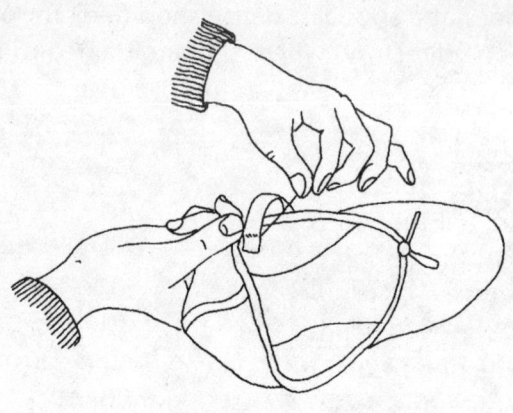

How do you tie ballet shoe ribbons?

- Put your foot flat on the floor and take hold of the ribbon on the inside of your ankle. Pass it over your foot, around the back of your ankle, and then across the front.

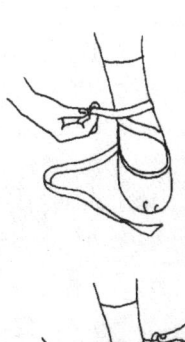

- Do the same with the outside ribbon, which should sit on top of the inside ribbon as you wrap it around your ankle.

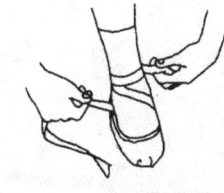

- Make sure that both ribbons are tight but comfortable and not restricting your foot movement.

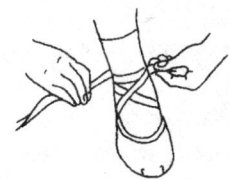

- Tie both ribbons in a double knot that sits on the inside (not the back!) of your ankle. There should be about 5 cm of ribbon left after the knot – if there is more, cut the ribbon to this length.

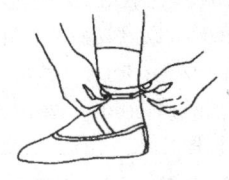

- Neatly tuck in the ends under the ribbon that is wrapped around your ankle.

SPOTLIGHTS

Ballet shoes are handmade. Each shoemaker has their own identity symbol which is stamped on the soles of the shoes they make — some dancers will only wear shoes made by one shoemaker as they find these the most comfortable! And dancers can get through lots of pairs. A pair of pointe shoes will last a professional only two or three weeks. A dancer who is performing a particularly demanding lead role, such as Giselle, *may even get through a couple of pairs a night. Each dancer in a ballet company is allocated a set number of shoes each month which are kept in a pigeon hole backstage with their name on.*

Do I have to wear tights?

Ballet practise clothes, such as leotards, are designed to be close-fitting so your teacher can clearly see your body. Most teachers like you to start with bare legs and ankle socks so they can see your muscles working correctly. Later both girls and boys wear tights because they are the best thing to cover your legs while allowing them to move completely freely. Girls usually wear pink tights so they blend in with their pink shoes and don't break the 'line' of the leg from the hip to the toe. Boys usually wear black tights for the same reason, though they sometimes wear white ankle socks over the top.

Why do professional ballet dancers always look so scruffy when they practise?

Because they wear the comfiest things they can find, which are often their oldest clothes! They also wear lots of layers so they can peel them off as their muscles warm up after the start of class and then layer them back on at the end so their muscles don't get cold. If you are cold, your teacher will probably prefer you to wear a cross-over cardigan and leg-warmers so that they can see your body clearly.

What about hair?

Ballet dancers spend a lot of time and practice trying to keep their head lifted and poised in beautiful lines, so it's important to be able to see it clearly. Both girls and boys should keep their hair off their face and away from their neck.

If you're a girl:
- Fix long hair in a bun or in plaits tied over your head.
- Short hair should be gripped back securely, perhaps with the help of a hairband or hairnet.

If you're a boy:
- Tie long hair back into a pony tail.

Romantic

Classical

Girls' Hairstyles

31

When do girls get to wear tutus?

If you are going to dance in a special performance, your teacher may suggest that you wear a tutu, which you can buy ready-made from a specialist shop. But you won't need a tutu for ballet class – it's best to practise in a plain leotard with perhaps a short ballet skirt over it, so your teacher can see your body clearly.

SPOTLIGHTS

Tutu much

In Romantic Ballets, girls wore soft, full skirts that fell nearly to the ankle. The first tutus appeared as skirts got shorter and shorter so that dancers could show off their clever leg and footwork to the audience. The skirt was stiffened and made more full. Nowadays, tutus are worn mostly in Classical Ballets.

Should I wear make-up or jewellery?

Not during class! For a start they are distractions which can stop either you or other people from watching what your body is doing. And jewellery can be dangerous if you or someone else accidentally catches it and pulls it. Save make-up for performances, when it will stop you looking pale under the bright stage lights. You might also have special stage jewellery which is in keeping with the character you are portraying.

Can I do exams or dance in shows?

There are different examination boards within ballet training and your teacher will be a member of at least one of them. An examination board (such as the Royal Academy of Dancing, the Cecchetti Society, the British Ballet Organisation, and the Imperial Society of Teachers of Dancing) will set the syllabus you follow in your class. All of them teach the same movements, although some of the positions of the arms and legs and *enchaînements* (sequences of steps) may have slightly different names.

Once you've started going to a ballet class, sooner or later you'll be put forward for an exam. Most people get nervous at exam time, but doing exams gives you a goal to work towards, an opportunity to show off what you've learnt, and a way to check your progress.

Your dancing school may also put on an annual show or you may be given the opportunity to perform in a local theatrical production. Occasionally a touring ballet company will audition local dancers for parts in a professional production such as *The Nutcracker*. Performing in a show gives you the chance to feel what it's like to learn and prepare a whole dance, and appear on stage in costume and make-up in front of an audience – just what ballet is all about!

SPOTLIGHTS

Dancers don't just make-up their faces, but often their bodies too for some ballets. In 'white' ballets where whole groups of girls dance together as ghosts or spirits, they will cover their arms, shoulders and neck in a thick white make-up called 'wet white', so their skin tones all look exactly the same. They might even cover their ballet shoes with it, to whiten the shiny pink satin!

'Wet pink' is sometimes used by ballerinas on their upper body to mask any redness or shine that might appear on their skin as they heat up through their strenuous dancing. It also stops any 'grip marks' appearing where partners have been holding them. All these things might distract people from watching their dancing.

4 Ballet basics

So you've found a teacher and a ballet class, you know what clothes to wear, and you're ready to get going . . . nearly! There are a few things that are really helpful to know (and practise) before you begin.

How do I hold myself?

- Always stand as tall and straight as you can. (It's very easy to forget and start to slouch!)
- Pull up all your leg muscles really tight, and tighten your tummy muscles and bottom (so that neither sticks out).
- Lift up out of your hips and hold your spine straight, with your shoulders down and slightly back.
- Lengthen out your neck, lifting your head but looking straight ahead.

Correct body positioning is known as placing. To keep your body placed correctly while you dance, imagine that there is a straight line running from the top of your head down the middle of your body to between your feet, and another straight line running across your hips. Try to keep these lines still while you move.

SPOTLIGHTS

Don't worry if you come across the name of a ballet step or phrase that you don't understand or can't pronounce! Just look it up in the glossary which is on pages 125-127.

SPOTLIGHTS

*Standing directly facing the front is known as standing
en face. Turning your body slightly at an angle to
en face is known as épaulement. Using épaulement
can really show off your head, neck and arm lines well.*

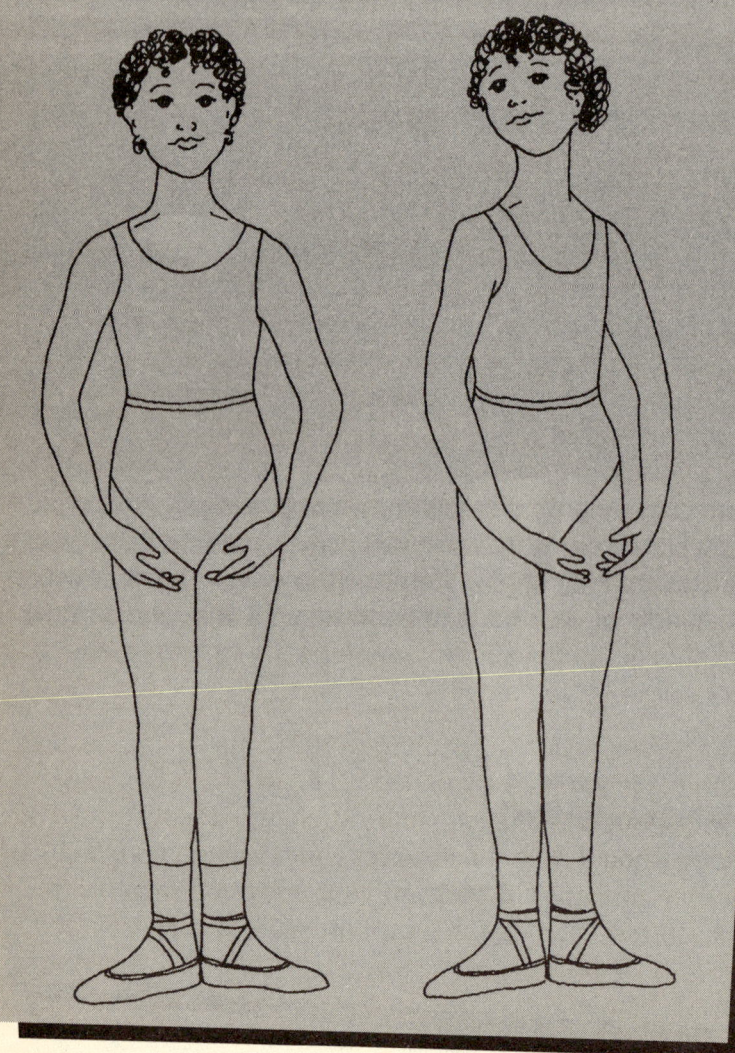

What's all this about turnout?

All ballet dancers work hard to turn their legs out from the top of the hip so their knees and feet face sideways instead of forwards – something that takes years of practice and must be learned under supervision.

It's all very well for you to laugh. You've got natural turnout.

When you first try it, you'll probably find that you can turn your feet out surprisingly well. However, if you check carefully, you'll most likely find that your knees are bent and still facing forwards, which means that you're cheating! You should only turn out your legs as far as you can comfortably when your legs are completely straight and pulled up. Your knees should always point over your toes and your feet should never roll inwards. As your body gets more used to this turned-out position, you'll gradually be able to rotate your legs further to the side while keeping the correct positioning and your weight placed evenly over both feet.

The five positions of the feet

All ballet steps are based on five foot positions, which are designed to keep your weight spread evenly for balance, and to give you a good base from which to jump high and land securely.

First (en première)
Stand with your legs turned out and your heels touching.

Second (en seconde)
Stand with your legs turned out and your feet apart. The space between your heels should be about one and a half times the length of your own foot. Keep your weight spread evenly over all of your toes.

Third (en troisième)
With your legs turned out, put the heel of one foot touching the middle of the other foot. (Don't forget to try it with the other leg in front too!) Spread your weight on both feet equally. You should be well turned-out and feel completely comfortable in this position before you try fifth position.

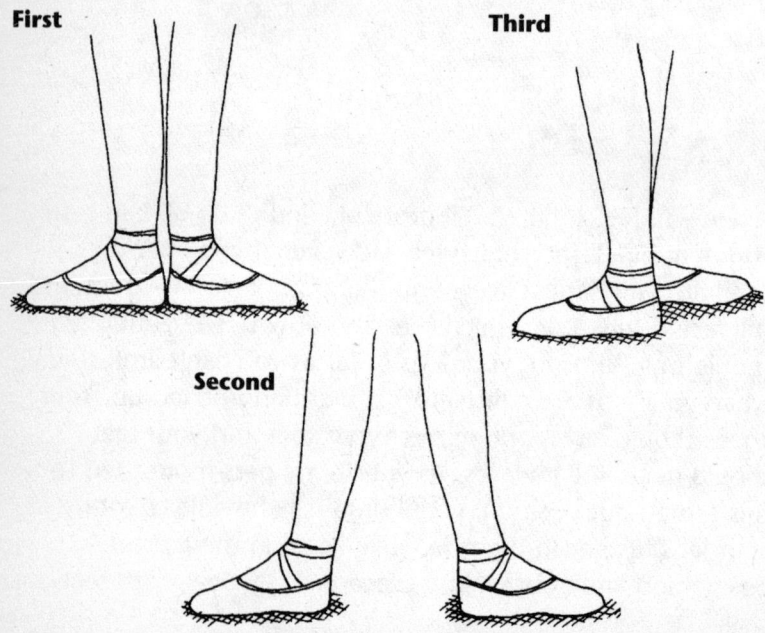

First

Third

Second

There are two fourth positions:

Open fourth/
Fourth opposite first
(en quatrième ouverte)

From first position, move one foot directly forward. The space between your feet should be about the length of one of your own feet.

Crossed fourth/
Fourth opposite fifth
(en quatrième croisée)

From fifth position (see below), move one foot directly forward. The space between your feet should be about the length of one of your own feet.

(You'll probably find that the fourth positions are the hardest, as it's difficult to turn out the legs correctly in these positions. Make sure that you don't try too hard and cause your feet to roll inwards.)

Fifth position
(en cinquième)

From third position, cross your front foot further over your back foot, until your heels are in line with your toes. (Be careful not to over-cross your feet.) You should only try this position when you've worked hard on your turnout and can comfortably master a well turned out third position.

Open Fourth

Fifth

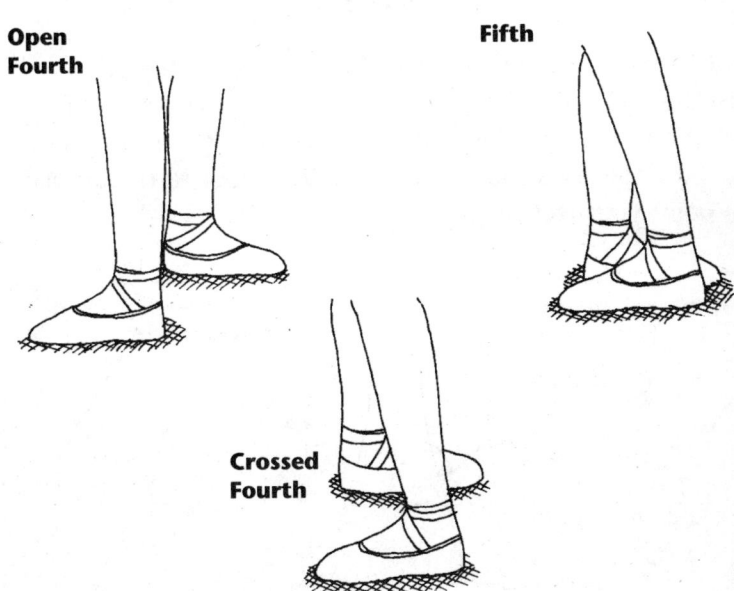

Crossed Fourth

How do I point my feet?

Pointing your feet is harder than you might think! When you first try to point your feet you might find that only your toes are curling over, rather than your whole foot stretching. Try not to think of bending or curling your foot, instead think of lengthening it out, from right across the ankle down your whole foot and along through to the tips of your toes.

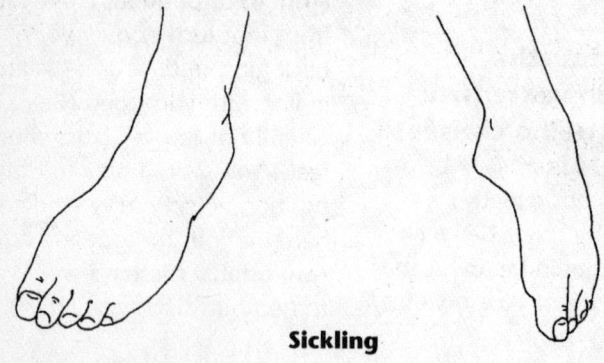

Sickling

You might also notice that your foot is curving inwards from the ankle, which is known as sickling. To correct this, stretch down both sides of the feet equally right through to your little toe. This should help you keep your turnout while you point your feet.

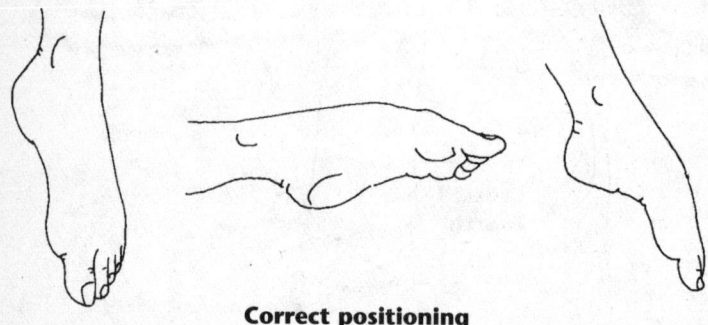

Correct positioning

As a ballet dancer, you should point your feet each time you move them or lift them off the floor, so your leg makes a beautiful line right down to the tips of your toes. Practising pointing your feet properly will also develop the strength you need in your feet and legs. One good exercise is to sit on the floor with your back up straight and legs together. Make sure that you keep your legs straight and your knees pulled up all the time. Pull your toes up to the ceiling and towards you, pressing down through your heels. Then point your feet down towards the floor. Repeat each position several times, holding for a few seconds each time, making sure you don't bend your knees.

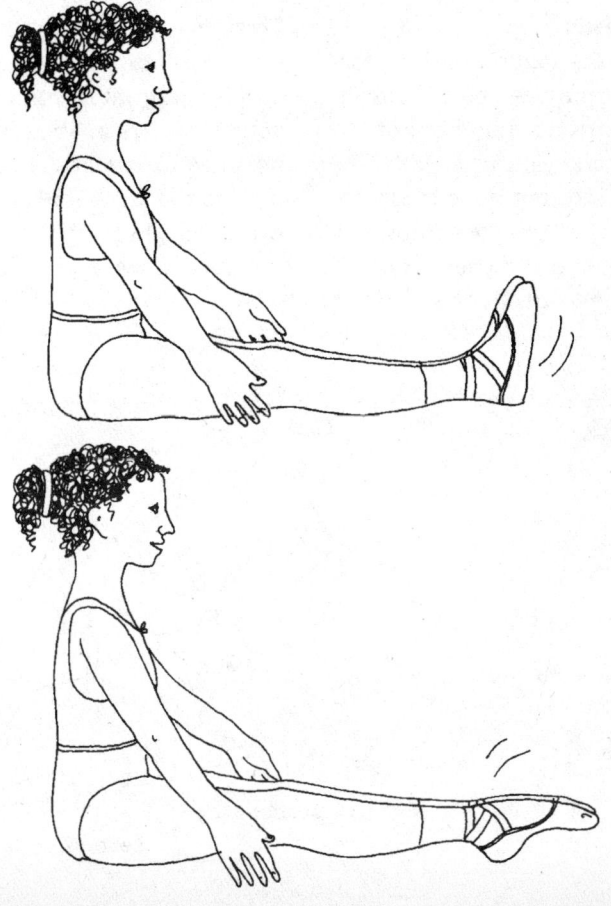

Basic arm positions

Ballet dancers use their arms in many different ways, but there are five basic positions you should learn at first. In all of these, you should try to make a long, curved shape with your arms, running smoothly from the top of your shoulder to the tips of your fingers. Concentrate on not dropping your elbows out of this line or letting your wrists stick out, which is known as 'breaking the line'. Hold your fingers in a delicate curve, with your thumbs relaxed and your middle fingers slightly more curved in than the rest. Try not to make your fingers either too spikey or too droopy.

Bras bas

This is the starting position for your arm movements. Hold your arms down in front of you in an oval shape, with your hands not quite touching your legs. Keep your elbows in a soft curve and your hands and fingers gently rounded.

First

From *bras bas*, move your arms up in front of you until your hands are at about waist height. You should still be making the same softly curved oval shape, keeping your shoulders down and your elbows lifted.

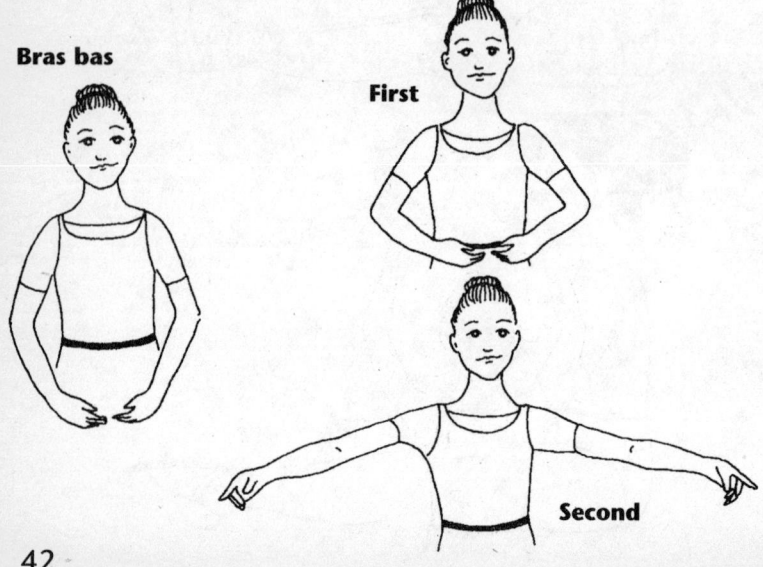

Bras bas

First

Second

Second

From first, open your arms out to the sides, keeping them in front of your shoulders.
(To check that you haven't taken your arms too far back, keep your head and eyes forwards, and you should still be able to see both of them.) You arms should still be curved, with your hands and fingers gently rounded. Be especially careful in this position that your elbows don't droop. Also concentrate on keeping your shoulders down and your head lifted.

Third

Hold one arm in first position and the other arm in second

position. Make sure that your back is straight and that you aren't rounding your shoulders. Also remember to keep your elbows lifted into line.

Fourth

With one arm in second position, hold the other one in a long, curved shape above your head and slightly in front of you.

Fifth

Hold both arms up above your head and slightly in front of you, making an oval shape that frames your face. Make sure that your shoulders stay down when you lift your arms.

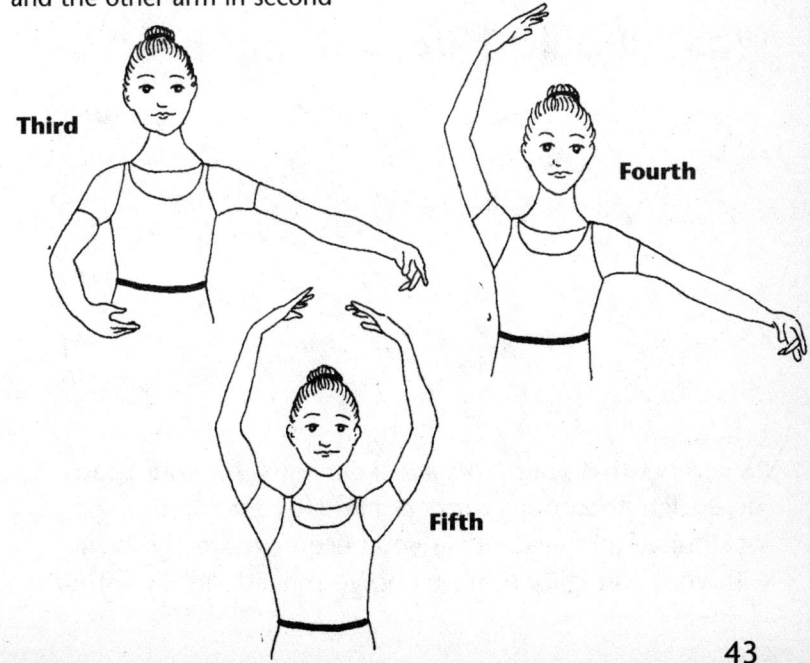

Third

Fourth

Fifth

Moving from one arm position to the next

Moving your arms from one position to the next is called *port de bras*. You will do special *port de bras* exercises in class to help you learn to move your arms gracefully. Imagine that your arms are light and delicate, and that you are moving them slowly through water instead of waving them about in the air. Don't make your arms too floaty by letting your hands lift and lower as you move your arms. Instead, try to keep your whole arm in a soft, curved line as you move. And when you're concentrating on your *port de bras*, don't forget about the rest of your body! Try to remember the tips on page 35. As you progress with your *port de bras*, your teacher might show you a second way to hold your fingers called *allongé*. In this position, you gently turn your palm downwards and softly open out your fingers.

What should I do with my head?

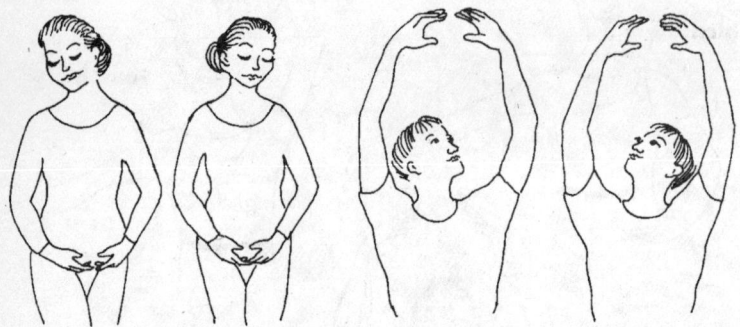

Remember that your arms are like a frame for your head. Always lengthen out your neck and lift your head so you look poised and elegant. As you become more confident with your *port de bras*, try tilting your head slightly within the shape of your arms. When you look up, always keep your neck long so your head doesn't drop back and out of line with the rest of your body. When you look down, always imagine that you're looking over something, so your chin doesn't sag on to your chest.

What happens at the barre?

The *barre* is a wooden pole that runs around the walls of the studio. It's used for all ballet warm-ups, and you will learn your first ballet exercises by holding on to it for balance, either facing the *barre* or with your side to it. (Try to avoid learning ballet with a teacher who uses the back of a chair instead of a *barre*.)

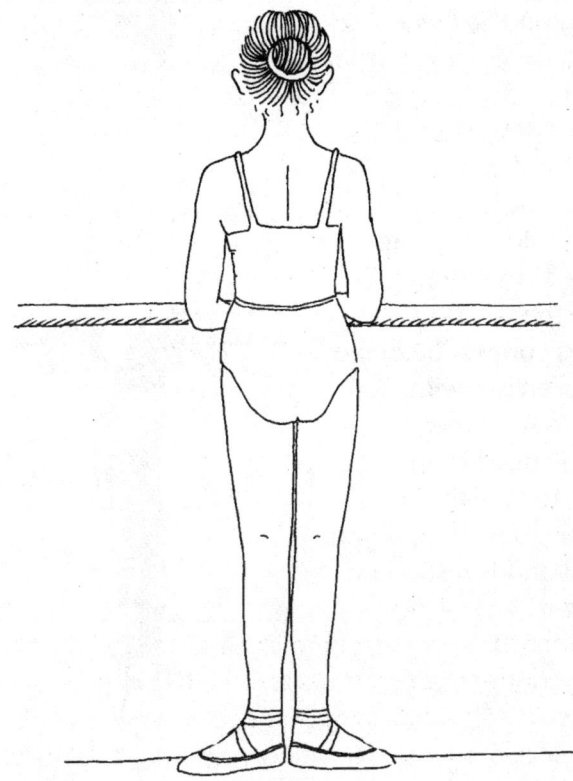

Ballet basics

- Always hold the barre lightly, resting your fingers and thumbs on top of it gently, rather than grabbing it.
- Don't lean on the *barre*. Try to find your own centre of balance and just use the *barre* as a light support if you wobble.
- Stand close enough so that you can reach the *barre* without bending forwards, but far enough away that your arms are relaxed when you rest your fingers on it – not uncomfortably bent or straight.
- When you're facing the *barre*, your hands should be shoulder-width apart.
- Remember to keep your shoulders down and relaxed.
- When you stand sideways at the *barre*, the hand resting on the *barre* should be slightly in front of you.
- The leg nearest to the *barre* is called the supporting leg.
- The leg closest to the centre of the room is called the working leg – the leg you will be doing your exercises with. To exercise the other leg, you will need to turn round to face the opposite direction so your other hand is resting on the *barre*.

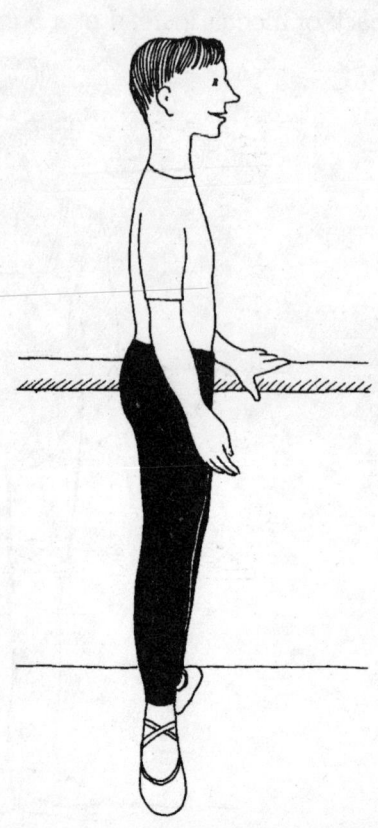

You will learn many movements by first facing the *barre*, then doing them again sideways on. While your legs are working, you should hold your free arm in second position. To 'prepare' your free arm, start with it in the *bras bas* position. As the music for the exercise starts, breathe in and lift your body up, gently opening your arm out to the side slightly from the fingertips. Then take your arm back through *bras bas* to first position, before opening it out to second position. Follow your arm movements with your head and, as you move, try to express what you feel as you hear the music.

Why warm up?

Like sportspeople, all dancers need to do special exercises to warm up. These get the joints moving smoothly and stretch the muscles out, so that you can move freely. If you don't warm up properly your muscles won't be ready to work at their best, so you'll find it difficult to balance and bend, to lift your legs, or to jump high. You may even injure yourself. No matter how advanced dancers may be, they always begin with the same warm-up exercises at the *barre*. Here are some of them to practise.

Pliés

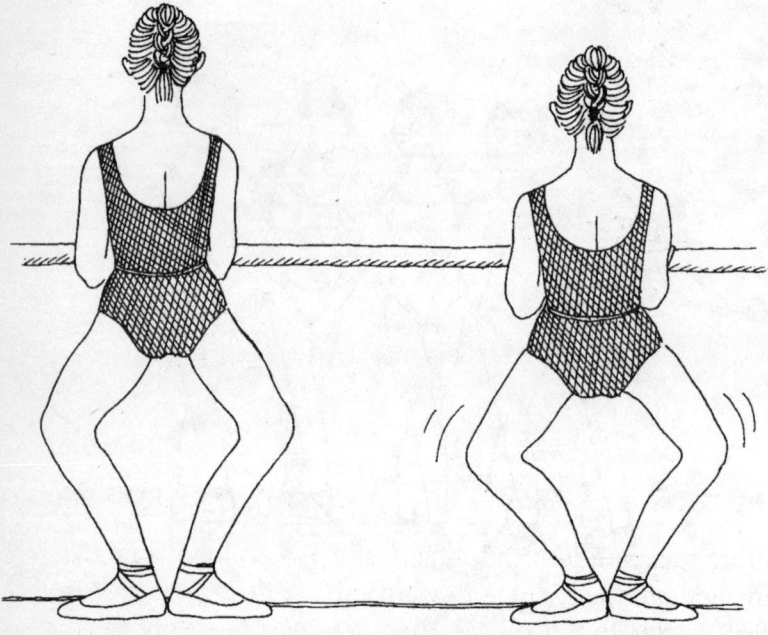

A ballet warm up involves different kinds of special turned-out knee bends called *pliés*. The first type of *plié* to practise is a *demi-plié*. Start facing the *barre* with your feet in first. Keeping your back and head up straight, with your shoulders and hips level, slowly bend your knees out over your toes, keeping your legs turned out from the hip. Go as far as you can, keeping your heels flat on the floor, then slowly straighten your legs again until your muscles are pulled up tight.

Practise doing *demi-pliés* in first, second and third position. (Your teacher will tell you when you're ready to try *pliés* in fourth and fifth position.) Watch that you don't bend your legs too far when you're in second position.

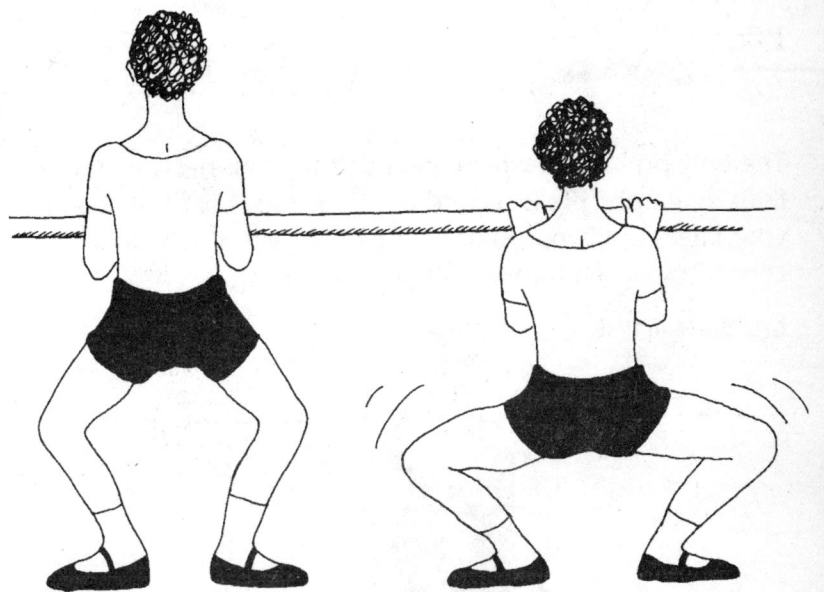

Once you can do a controlled *demi-plié*, your teacher will include *grand pliés* in your warm up. To do a *grand plié* in first, start with a *demi-plié*, then gradually peel your heels off the floor as you bend your legs until your thighs are parallel with the floor. Be sure to stop in this position, so you don't end up sitting on your heels! On the way up, replace your heels as soon as you can without straining.

Ballet basics

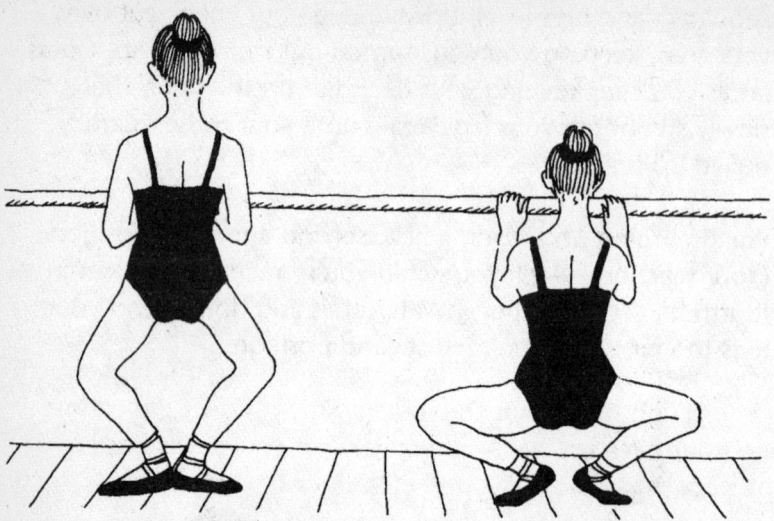

The only position in which you don't lift your heels off the floor in a *grand plié* is second position. You should still bend your knees until your thighs are parallel with the floor, concentrating on turning out your whole leg.

Grand plié in first

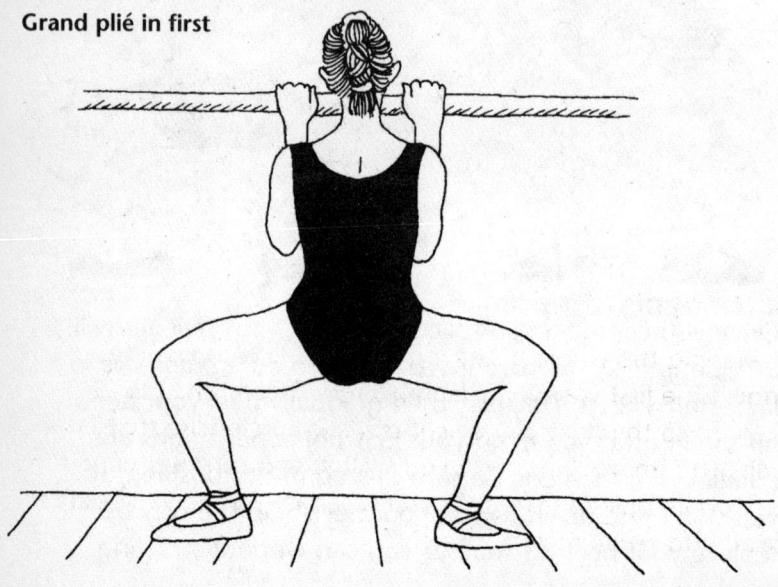

Relevés

A ballet warm up includes lots of exercises to loosen and strengthen your ankles and feet, such as rising up on to the balls of your feet. You can rise, or *relevé* in every position of the feet. Make sure your weight is spread over your whole foot before you begin. Then, keeping your turnout and all your leg muscles pulled up tight, raise both heels off the floor at the same time until you are balanced on the balls of your feet as high as you can go, a position known as *demi-pointe*. Remember to lift your body up out of your hips so you feel light and tall, with your tummy muscles pulled in and your back straight. Gradually lower your heels back to the floor, making sure your feet are neatly in position.

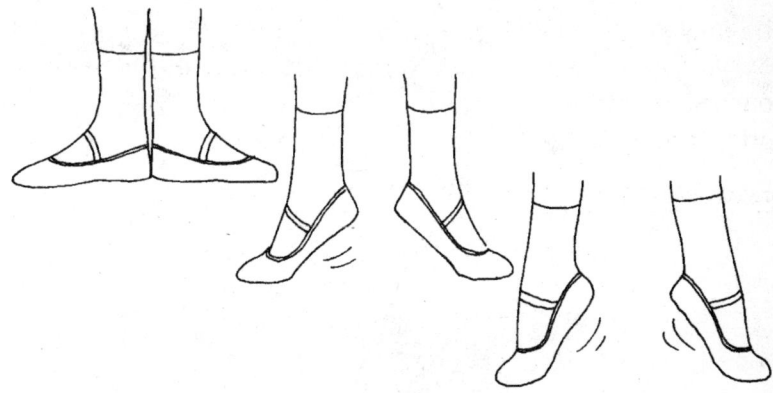

Battements tendus

Stretching the whole of the leg and sliding it across the floor is the first way you'll learn to move from one foot position to the next. *Battement tendu* is an exercise that helps you improve the way you stretch and turn out your legs, while building strength and balance. *Battement* means 'beat' and *tendu* means 'stretch'.

Ballet basics

Stand with your side to the *barre* and your feet in first position. Keeping your weight straight over your supporting leg, slide your working leg straight forwards, leading first with your heel and then with your toes, until your foot is pointed. After you have stretched your leg and foot fully, slowly draw your leg back to first position, turning your toes and foot out first and gradually replacing your whole foot on to the floor. Stretching your leg forwards like this is called a *battement tendu devant*.

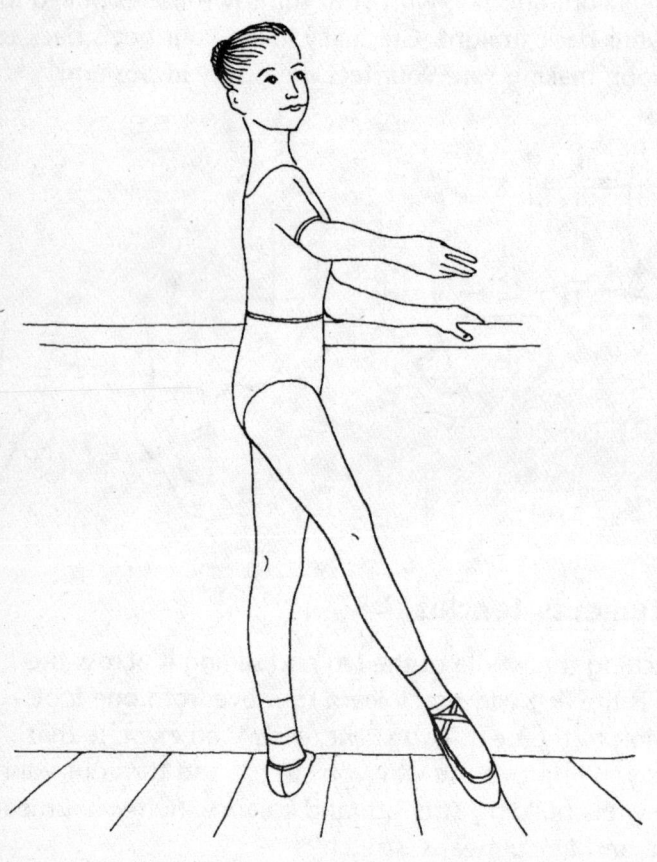

A *battement tendu à la seconde* is done the same way as a *battement tendu devant,* but to the side instead of to the front. Work hard on turning out your leg from the hip in this exercise, so your knees and toes point sideways in a line.

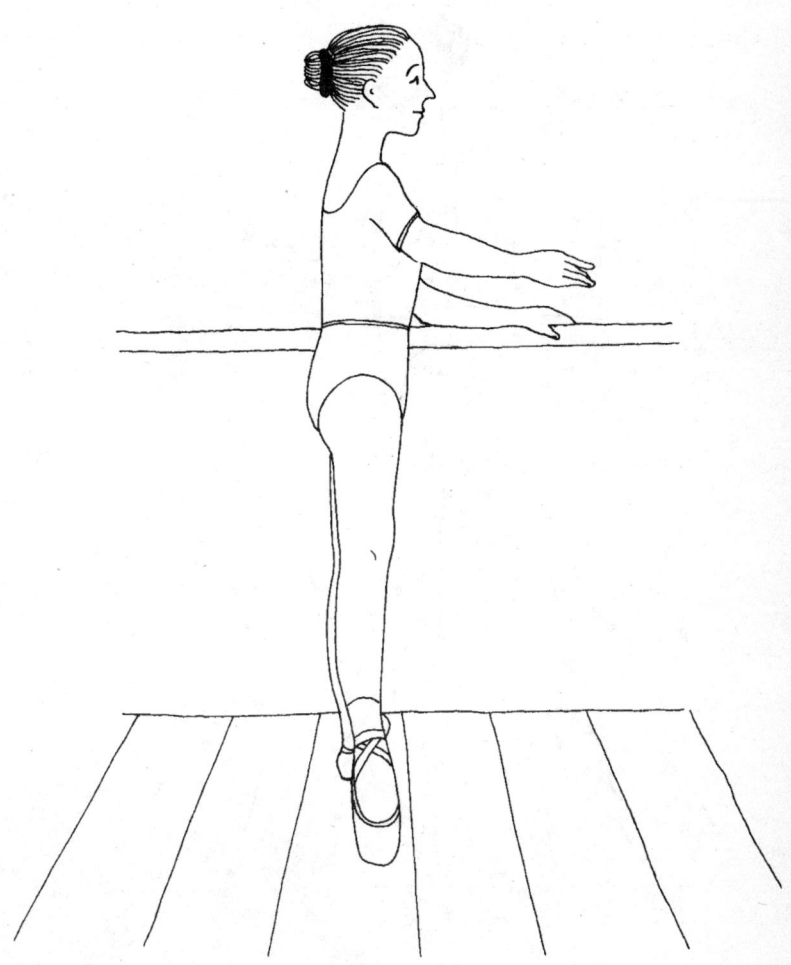

Ballet basics

A *battement tendu derrière* goes behind you. Be careful to keep your back up straight when you perform this exercise, so you don't lean forwards. Also watch out that you don't lift the hip of your working leg as you try to turn your leg out while sliding it backwards. Keep both hips square to the front and level with the floor.

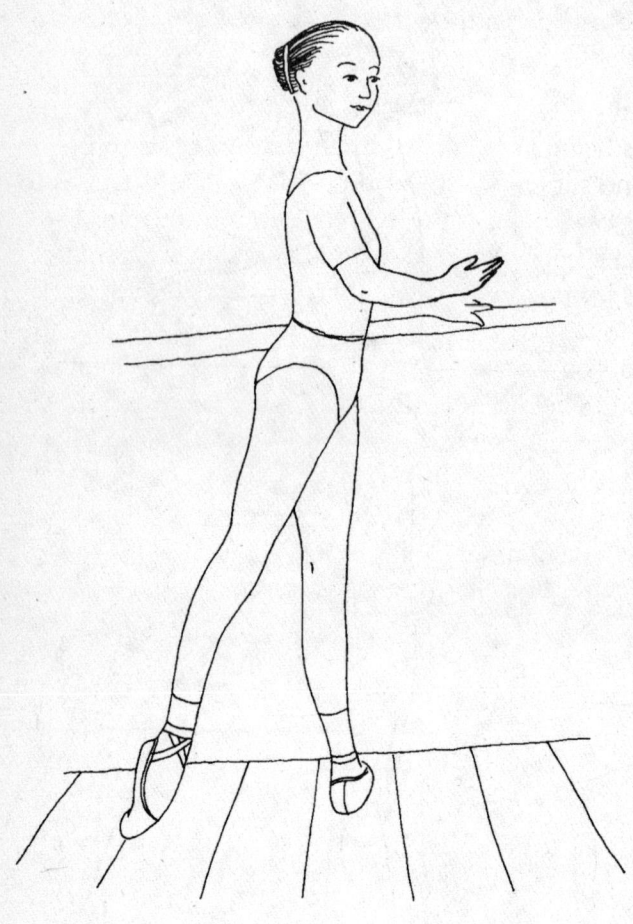

During a *battement tendu* your foot should not leave contact with the ground. You should feel your whole foot pushing through the floor as you point it. Once you have practised *battement tendus* starting from first position, you can warm up with *battement tendus* starting from third and also fifth position. The cross shape you make by turning out your supporting leg, and moving your working leg to the front, side and behind, is called *en croix*.

Bending

As well as being very strong, ballet dancers need to be flexible and supple. Your warm up will include exercises to help your back bend easily, with a flowing movement. Always keep your neck and head in line with your spine, and bend from the waist without pushing your hips and stomach forwards. Keep your legs well turned out and the muscles pulled up tight. Don't hold your breath! Breathe out as you bend, and breathe in as you straighten up.

What happens at the end of the class?

Get ready to thank your teacher at the end of each class by practising a special bow called a *révérence*.

- For girls, this is a bit like a curtsey, as you point one foot behind the other and bend both knees in *demi-plié*.
- Boys stand straight and incline their head politely.

 Moving on – at the barre

As you get better at holding your turnout and keeping your body placed correctly, and as your balance and strength improves, your teacher will give you new exercises to try at the *barre*. You'll do many of these exercises again later on in class, in the centre of the room. Don't be dismayed if you seem to be progressing very slowly. Being good at ballet involves going over the same exercises again . . . and again . . . and again. . . Try harder each time to make your movements perfect. Even if you one day become a professional ballet dancer, you will still find yourself doing these same exercises, day after day, for all the years of your dancing career. Every time you perform an exercise – no matter how simple it is – concentrate on doing it as well as you can, and on showing your feelings about the movement and the music through your dancing.

SPOTLIGHTS

You could ask to have a mini barre of your own in your bedroom – made out of a piece of broom handle which is attached to the wall!

What else can I do at the barre?

Rond de jambes à terre

This exercise is good for improving your turnout. It draws a semi-circle on the ground ('on the ground' is what *à terre* means) and you can do the movement two ways: either circling it *en dehors* (outwards) or *en dedans* (inwards).

Moving on – at the barre

Begin by stretching your working leg to second position (like the first movement in *battement tendu à la seconde*).

To move *en dehors*, sweep your leg behind you, gliding your pointed toes across the floor and keeping your leg straight and turned out.

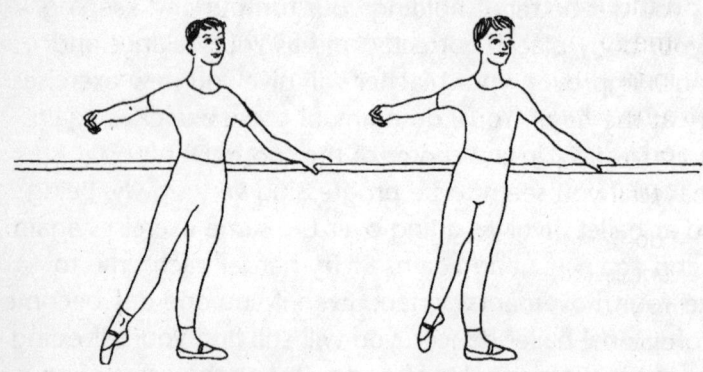

Close your leg to first (as you would in *battement tendu derrière*), then stretch it forwards (as you would in the first movement of a *battement tendu devant*).

Finally sweep your stretched leg and foot out to your starting position in second, to complete the semi-circle.

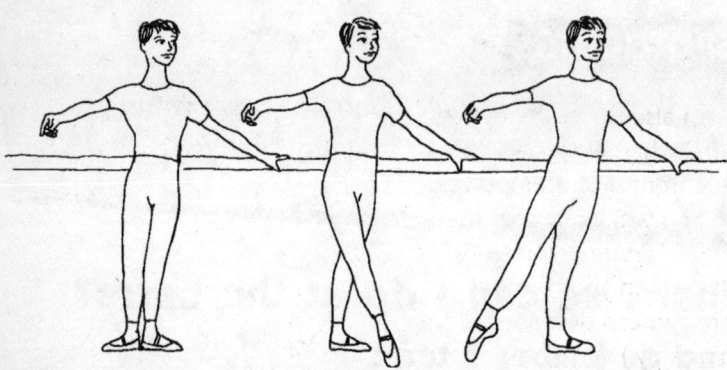

Throughout this exercise, hold your arm elegantly in second position, keeping all your weight balanced over your supporting leg, and your shoulders and hips square to the front. To circle the leg *en dedans*, from second, sweep your leg in front of you and reverse the direction of the semi-circle.

Battements fondus

Through this exercise you'll develop great control over your muscles. It will also help you to dance with feeling, listening carefully to the music and matching your movements in time. In this exercise, both legs work together at exactly the same time to 'melt' down (the meaning of *fondu*) and rise up again in a perfectly smooth and continuous flow. To perform *battement fondu* you'll need to know how to hold your working foot against your supporting ankle, or *sur le coup de pied*:

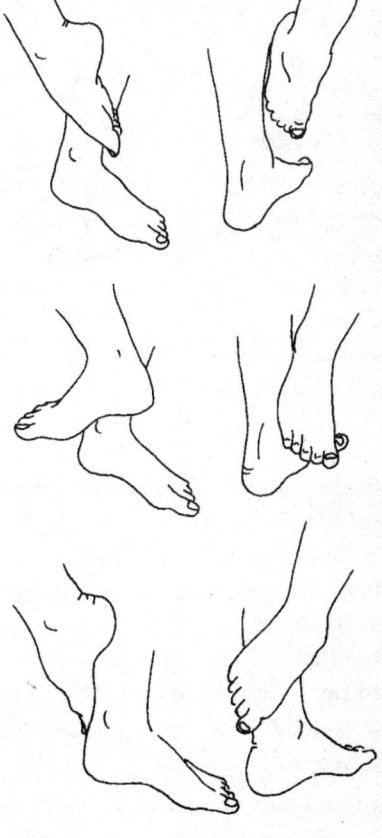

You can do this with a pointed foot *devant* (in front) by stretching your working foot and holding the tip of your toe against the ankle bone of your supporting foot.

Or you can do this with a flexed foot *devant* by flattening your working foot and holding the heel against the ankle bone of your supporting foot.

You can also do this 'wrapped around' where your heel is held in front of the supporting ankle and you wrap your toes behind it. (You may need to work hard on your turnout before you can do this comfortably.)

Begin *battement fondu* in fifth position, with your working leg in front of your supporting leg.

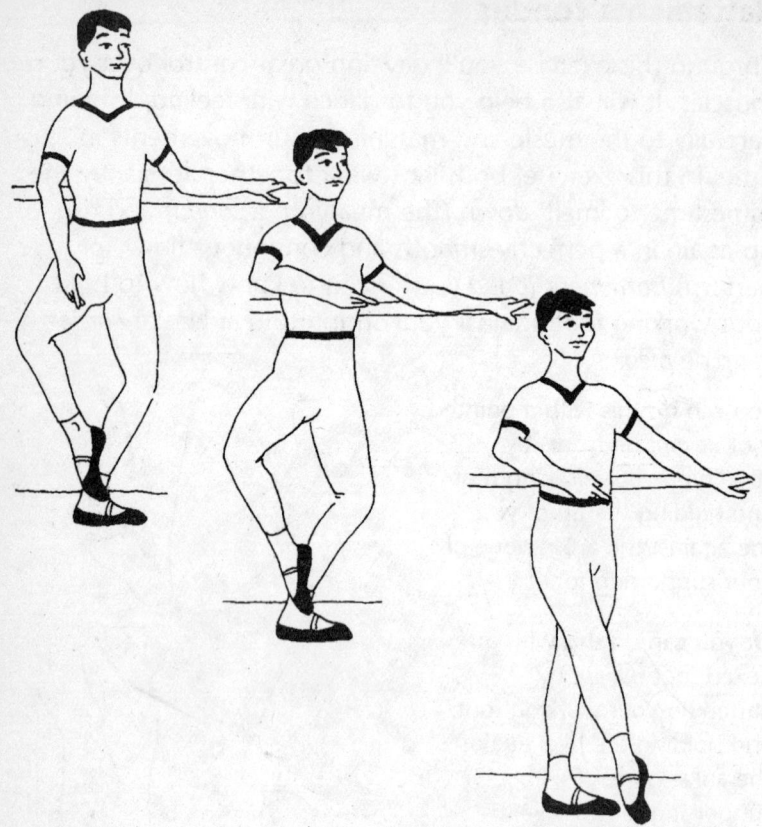

Peel up your working heel and lift your foot off the floor, keeping both legs fully turned out, and beginning to bend both knees at exactly the same time.

'Melt' towards the floor by bending your supporting leg to *demi-plié* at the same time as you raise your working foot to a pointed *cou de pied devant*.

Slowly straighten your supporting leg at the same time as you unfold your working leg from the knee until your leg and foot are stretched in front of you into *dégagé devant*. (Unfold your arm to first position at the same time.)

Repeat the 'melting' part of the exercise, and this time unfold your working leg to the side *à la seconde*. (Unfold your arm the same way.)

Repeat the 'melting' part of the exercise once again, but this time take your working foot to a pointed *cou de pied derrière*. As you straighten your supporting leg, unfold your working leg behind you, *derrière*. (Lengthen your arm to an *arabesque* line in front of you; *arabesques* are explained in the next chapter.)

Throughout the exercise, stay well turned out with your hips level. Keep the movement steady and flowing, with both legs reaching the final points of the bend and stretch at the same time.

Preparation for battements frappés

Battement frappé is a much faster movement than the three previous *barre* exercises described above. *Frapper* means 'to strike', and you should aim for speed and power in this exercise.

Begin with your working foot flexed *sur le cou de pied devant*.

Keeping your thigh still, stretch out your lower leg quickly (going through the foot) and powerfully to second position, pointing your foot.

Keeping your thigh still, return your working foot swiftly to *cou de pied*, but this time *derrière*. Your foot should not touch the floor as you bend in your leg.

Your movements should be precise and with even force throughout. When you are used to doing this action in a well turned-out position, with strength and accuracy, you can progress on to a proper *battement frappé*: the ball of your working foot strikes the floor sharply as you extend your leg, until your foot points just off the floor. Your working leg returns to *cou de pied* sharply, but with less force. (Never swing your working leg; always stretch it precisely and powerfully.)

Petits battements

This means 'small beat', and will develop your speed and
neatness. Hold your arm down in *bras bas* throughout.

Begin with your working leg
sur le cou de pied devant (your
foot can be pointed, flexed or
wrapped around).

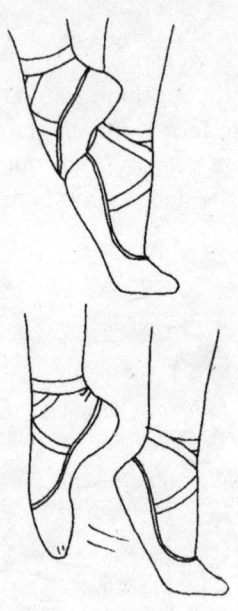

Keeping your thigh turned out
and still, move your working
foot slightly to the side,
strongly and precisely.

Quickly and accurately, return
your working foot to the *cou
de pied* position, this time
derrière. (Repeat the
movement again to take your
foot back to the front,
devant.)

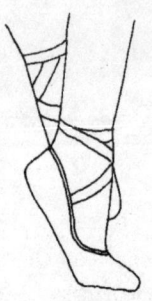

After some practice, your teacher will ask you to try *petits
battements* with your supporting leg pulled up to *demi-pointe*.
Concentrate on lifting your body, tightening your stomach and
leg muscles, and finding your centre of balance.

Développés

This exercise involves unfolding the leg into a beautiful line. You must keep your supporting leg well pulled up, and your body lifted and still as your working leg moves. Only lift your leg as high as you can under control, keeping your turnout, and holding your hips level. (Use your arms in the same way as for *battement fondu*.)

Begin in third or fifth position. Lift your working leg through *cou de pied* until your toe touches your knee. This is the *retiré* position.

Unfold your leg in front of you as high as you can while keeping your turnout and not letting any part of you move out of line.

Lower your leg and close it through *battement tendu*.

Do this exercise *en croix*, extending your leg in front of you, to the side, and behind. You won't be able to unfold your leg very high at first, but if you work hard, you'll later be able to hold it at waist height or even higher.

65

Grands battements

Do this big, sweeping, high-kick movement *en croix* to improve your suppleness and balance. (Hold your arm steadily in second position.)

Start in third or fifth position. Stretch your leg quickly and powerfully through *battement tendu* and carry on sweeping your leg up off the floor. (Make sure your hips stay level, that your supporting leg doesn't bend, and that your body stays erect. Don't forget to point your foot all the time!)

Lower your leg back down to the ground with control so it doesn't just drop to the floor, and close it through *battement tendu*.

Perfection Pointers

Rond de jambes à terre

You will move on to *rond de jambe en l'air*, where the circular action is performed with the leg off the ground. The movement is performed from the knee, while holding the thigh completely still. It is a good way to warm-up for slow and controlled exercises involving stretching the leg high.

Battements fondus

You will progress to learning *battement fondu en l'air*, where you keep your working leg off the ground when you stretch it out. Though you have to work hard to keep your body straight and your hips level, some dancers achieve an angle of more than 90° between their lifted leg and the floor, while dancing the movement with feeling, grace and control. You will eventually learn to rise up on to *demi-pointe* or even full *pointe* as you extend your working leg, in the centre as well as at the *barre*.

Petit battements frappé

At some stage you'll combine *petit battement* and *battement frappé* so that you beat and strike from the *cou de pied* position while your supporting leg is pulled up on *demi-pointe*.

Développés

Work towards unfolding your leg higher while keeping correct placing. Dancers of an advanced standard perform *développés* not only in the centre, but also on *demi-* or full *pointe*.

Grands battements

These can also be performed as a slow raise and lower of the straight leg – which actually involves more control than sweeping the leg quickly. This strength-building way of performing the movement is called *relevé lent*. Once you have confidence at the *barre*, you can practise *grands battements* and *relevés lents* in the centre, too.

SPOTLIGHTS

Some professional ballet companies allow the public in to watch dress rehearsals on stage. The dancers often do a warm-up class on stage before the rehearsal begins which is a great chance to see real dancers going through the same steps you do at the barre! Why not phone up the nearest ballet company to where you live and ask about arrangements for rehearsals? You will find the telephone number in your local telephone directory.

Moving on – centrework

After working at the *barre* you will move into the centre of the studio, where you can practise the movements you have learnt, such as *pliés*, without anything to hold on to for support. You will use these movements to make beautiful ballet poses in different directions.

How do I know where to face?

Imagine that there is a square on the floor around your feet. Facing you, at the front of the square, is your audience. The square is divided up by lines running across it from each side and from the corners. You are standing in the centre of the square, exactly where all the lines cross in the middle. You can create different shapes and feelings for your audience by turning your body each way along these lines and positioning your legs differently. Practise holding your arms in different positions and looking out to your audience.

Croisé means 'crossed', and in *croisé* poses your legs look crossed to your audience. Turn your body to face a front corner of your square.

• For *croisé devant*, stretch the leg nearest your audience in front of you.

69

Moving on – centrework

- For *croisé derrière*,
  stretch the leg farthest
  away from your
  audience behind you.

In ballet *effacé* means
'open'. Again face a front
corner of your square.

- For *effacé devant*, stretch
  the leg farthest away
  from your audience in
  front of you.

- For *effacé derrière*,
  stretch the leg nearest
  your audience behind
  you.

Ecarté means 'wide apart'. Instead of stretching your leg in front or behind you, it involves stretching your leg to second, either towards or away from your audience. Standing on a diagonal and stretching your leg to second gives your body a completely flat, wide open, shape. Once more, face a front corner of your square.

- For *ecarté devant*, stretch the leg nearest to your audience to second.

- For *ecarté derrière*, stretch the leg farthest away from your audience to second.

Adage

Some centre exercises are known as *adage* work, where you try to make one movement flow as smoothly into the next as you can. *Adage* exercises require the most balance and control.

Arabesques

In an *arabesque*, a dancer makes a beautiful, long, straight line from the tips of the fingers, down through the arm and body, along the leg to the toes. There are many different types of *arabesque*, but the basic position you should practise first is *arabesque à terre*.

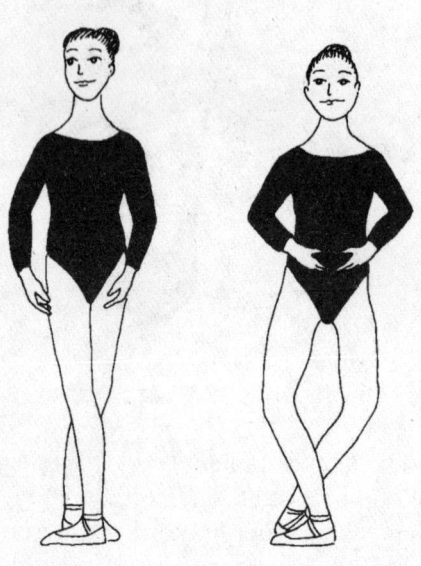

Start in third or fifth position with your arms *bras bas,* then slowly *demi-plié* and take your arms to first.

Slide your front foot into fourth position, still keeping your *demi-plié*.

Continuing to move smoothly, straighten your front leg and transfer your weight on to it, stretching your back leg out behind you. Stretch the same arm as your front leg out in front of you, fingers *allongé* (see page 44), with your other arm out to the side in line with your shoulder. You should hold the muscles in your back strongly, and look along the line of your front arm without leaning forwards. As your *arabesque* line improves, your teacher will tell you to practise opening out your side arm a little more.

73

Perfection Pointers

Second arabesque à terre

This is the next line to master, in which your front arm is the opposite to your front leg, rather than the same.

Third arabesque

In this line both arms stay in front of you, with the same arm as your front leg held higher than the other. As with all *arabesque* arm positions, don't drop your fingers or thumbs too much so you break the line, and make sure you keep your elbows lifted.

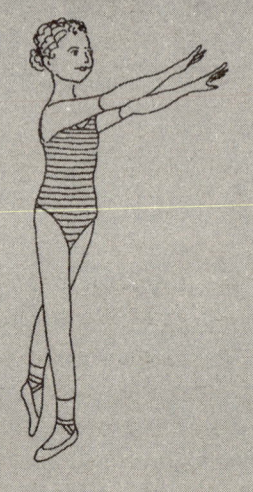

Arabesque en l'air

Eventually you will then try an *arabesque en l'air*, where you lift your leg behind you. Only lift your leg as high as you can without twisting your hip up; although both hips will tilt forwards slightly, they should still be level. You will need to have practised bending exercises to have developed the right amount of flexibility and strength in  your spine for this position. Keep your tummy and chest lifted, so you don't lean forwards as you lift your leg. Use your head and eyes to express the elegance of the line you feel through your body.

Arabesque penchée

After a lot of work you will be ready to try this most difficult type of *arabesque*. It involves holding your upper back strongly to keep the line of your *arabesque* steady while you tilt forwards and raise your leg higher than a 90° angle behind you. This is one of the most beautiful movements in ballet, but it takes years of practice!

Attitudes

An *attitude* is another *adage* position involving balancing on one leg. The leg can be bent either in front or behind you, with different arm positions. (When you lift your leg *en attitude* behind you, make sure that your toe is never higher than your knee.) *Attitudes* are used a lot in partner work, for instance, in turns and lifts.

How do the ballet steps link?

It's no good being brilliant at different ballet positions if you can't link them altogether into a flowing, expressive dance. You should try to show what you're feeling even when you run. A run in ballet is not like running normally. It's called *pas couru*. Girls should take tiny steps on *demi-pointe* with their legs pulled up, while 'presenting' their movement with their arms. On the other hand, boys should stretch out their legs and feet when they run, trying to cover as much ground as they can with each step.

Not all linking steps are fast, like *pas couru*. Some are slow and gliding; others are lifted and precise. Try to express the different natures of the steps when you dance them, bringing out the variety in their rhythms.

Glissades

This is a gliding step that you will probably first learn sideways, though you can also do it going forwards and backwards. As well as linking slow and controlled steps together it is also often used to lead into a leap. You should try to hold your *demi-plié* position throughout and work hard to feel your foot all along the floor in your *battement tendu*.

Begin in third or fifth position and bend to a *demi-plié*.

Moving on – centrework

Through *battement tendu*
stretch either your front or
back foot out to *dégagé* in
second just a fraction off the
floor, keeping your supporting
leg in *demi-plié*.

Transfer your weight onto the
leg you are stretching,
bending it into *demi-plié* and
stretching out your other leg
into *dégagé* in second just a
fraction off the floor. (You
should now be in exactly the
same position as in the second
movement of this step, but
using the other leg.)

Close your stretched leg
through *battement tendu* back
to where you started in third
or fifth, keeping low in your
demi-plié.

Bourrées

There are several different types of *bourrée*, each involving changing your weight quickly from one foot to the other three times. Try to be especially neat and light when you dance them.

To perform a *pas de bourrée piqué*, begin in a *demi-plié* in third or fifth position *sur le cou de pied derrière*.

Pull up your leg muscles quickly and lift your body, stepping on to your back leg on *demi-pointe* and picking up your front leg to *retiré*. (Be careful not to travel at this point – just replace one foot with the other.)

Change legs again on the spot by stepping on to your front leg on *demi-pointe* and lifting your other leg to *retiré*.

With the leg that is *retiré*, step down into a *demi-plié*, peeling the other leg off the floor to *cou de pied derrière*.

Piqué means 'pricked', and the sharp pricking movements of this step come from replacing one foot exactly with the other, so both feet are never on the ground at the same time.

Perfection Pointers

Pas couru

Girls eventually perform these tiny running steps on *pointe*. They can cover a great deal of the floor while looking as if their feet are hardly moving.

Glissades

Glissades à la seconde can be performed with a change of feet. Starting with the front foot and closing it to the back is called a *glissade* under. Starting with the back foot and closing it to the front is called a *glissade* over.

Pas de bourrée piqué

This is another step that girls dance on *pointe*, after perfecting it on *demi-pointe*.

How do I spin round without falling over?

If you've been to see a ballet, one thing you're sure to remember is the exciting turning. There are many different spins in ballet, and you will learn those that stay on the spot, called *pirouettes*, before trying those which travel, such as *piqué* turns and *chaîné* turns. Pirouettes can begin from different positions, with the working leg held either *sur le cou de pied*, in *retiré*, or even extended out straight (this is extremely difficult to do properly). With all types of pirouette it's possible to turn in two directions: *en dehors* (outwardly or backwards) and *en dedans* (inwardly or forwards).

en dehors   **en dedans**

There are two things you will need to practise to prepare for *pirouettes*: 'spotting' and *relevés*.

Spotting

This is a technique dancers use to stop themselves getting dizzy. As their body turns, they keep looking at the same spot in front of them for as long as they can. When they can no longer keep their head in that position, they whip their head round as quickly as possible to look back at the same spot. If you watch a dancer performing *pirouettes*, it looks as if their head is the last thing to leave their starting position and the first thing to get back to it! Practise shuffling round on the spot while you get the feeling of 'spotting' with your eyes and head. Don't forget to try it in both directions!

Relevés

Performing *relevés* in the centre will improve your strength and balance. You will not be able to turn until you can balance quite confidently on one leg on *demi-pointe*. So practise *relevés* if you want to avoid falling over a lot later!

Begin in a fifth *demi-plié* with your arms in third (same arm in front of you as your front leg).

Lift up on your back leg to *demi-pointe* and raise your front leg strongly to *retiré* simultaneously. (Move your outstretched arm into first position with a definite, positive movement.) Think upwards, as if someone is pulling you towards the ceiling from the very top of your head, but make sure you don't raise your shoulders. Your supporting leg and tummy muscles needs to be pulled up very tight. You may find that your centre of balance is a little further forwards over your supporting leg than you at first think. You will know when you have found it as you will feel perfectly balanced, without wobbling. Once you've found your centre of balance, the length of time you can stay pulled up in that position depends on your strength.

Close your working leg behind you from *retiré* to a fifth, sinking down smoothly into a *demi-plié*. Concentrate on spreading your weight evenly over both feet so you feel secure as you lower, and not as if you're about to over-balance.

SPOTLIGHTS

FOUETTÉS

A fouetté is a highly-exciting type of spin where a dancer whips their leg out and in while they turn. Girl dancers perform these on pointe, *keeping exactly on the same spot while they spin again . . . and again . . . and again . . . In some ballets, the ballerina has to perform as many as 32* fouettés *without stopping! (Now you can see why spotting is so important!) If you go to see* Swan Lake, *try counting how many* fouettés *the* Black Swan *performs – if she's not too fast for you!*

Perfection Pointers

When you first practise a proper *pirouette*, try not to think at all about turning. Concentrate on pulling up your leg, bottom and tummy muscles really tight, and lift your body upwards over your centre of balance rather than throwing your weight forwards or backwards as you go round. You must pull up with your hips and shoulders square to the front before you begin to turn.

Start off by perfecting a single turn before you attempt to spin round twice or three times. If you're a girl, don't ever be tempted to try a *pirouette* on *pointe* until you've practised special *barre* and centre exercises with your teacher. If you're a boy, you'll eventually learn how to finish your spins with a striking pose, such as lowering on to the floor on one knee. Finally, don't forget to practise turning each way, on each leg – or you'll end up brilliant at some types of *pirouette* and terrible at others!

7 Moving on – allegro

Movements in the centre which involve jumping are called *allegro* exercises, an Italian musical term meaning lively and quick. You will begin with small, neat jumps called *petit allegro* and progress to larger travelling leaps called *grand allegro* – the dynamic climax of the class. Both boys and girls need neat and precise leg and footwork, so you can perform steps that change legs in the air several times. Steps like this are called *batterie*, meaning beaten. Boys also need to develop the height and power of their jumping, while girls need to work on seeming light and graceful.

How do I prepare for jumping?

Just as the harder you press down a sponge, the faster it springs back, the more you bend in *demi-plié*, the higher you will be able to jump! Push down through your whole foot, especially your heels, keeping well turned out. If you're using your whole foot correctly, as you spring into the air, your foot should peel away from the floor with the tips of your toes leaving the ground last.

Moving on – allegro

When you jump, your legs
and feet should be neatly
positioned together and
perfectly stretched in the air.
Lift your body up, but be
careful not to throw it
backwards. Keep your
shoulders down and arms
relaxed, with a poised head
position. Jump as high as
you can while making it
look easy.

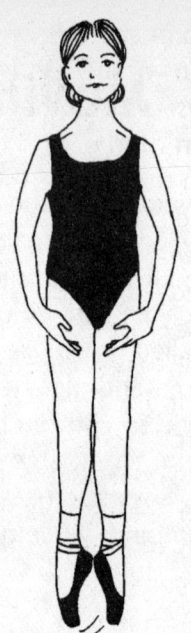

Use the whole of your foot
to make a smooth landing,
lowering through your toes
first, then along the length
of the foot, before pushing
the heels into the ground
and bending into a soft
demi-plié. Keep your back up
straight and your body and
head lifted. Watch that you
don't bob up from your
demi-plié between jumps;
sink down into it and use
every muscle in your legs to
spring up for the next jump.
(If you have finished your
movement, show this by
drawing your legs up
straight and tight together,
standing as tall as you can.)

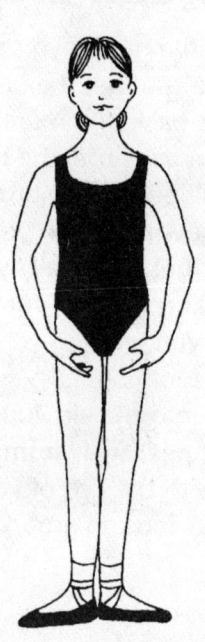

A jump in any one of the five positions of the feet is called a *temps levé*. A jump which starts in third or fifth, and ends in third or fifth with the other leg in front, is called a *changement*. (You should pull your legs up so tightly together that it looks as if you only have one leg when you're in the air. Be careful not to over-cross them, though! Draw the front leg up over the back leg on the way up, and bring the back leg to the front on the way down.)

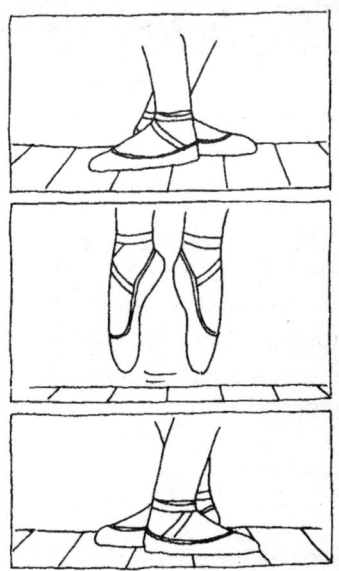

SPOTLIGHT

Rosin is a white powder made from the sap of fir trees. If you are dancing on a slippery wooden floor, rubbing a little rosin on to the toes and soles of your ballet shoes will help to stop you sliding and losing your grip.

Petit échappés sautés

This is a small, low jump from one of the five foot positions to another. The first type of *échapée sautée* to try is from fifth to second.

Demi-plié in fifth position to prepare for the jump, arms *bras bas*.

As you jump, stretch your legs to second position in the air. Don't forget to stretch your feet!

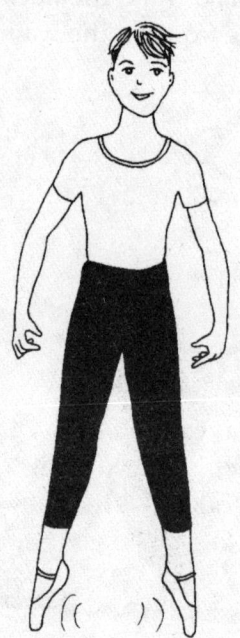

Land in a *demi-plié* in second position, and use this bend to help you spring straight back up to a stretched second position in the air.

Land in fifth with the other leg in front, and sink down into your *demi-plié*.

Pas de chats

Pas de chat means literally 'step of the cat'!

Begin in *demi-plié* in fifth position, with your arms in third (same arm in front as the leg behind), looking over your bent elbow slightly with your head lifted.

Peel your back foot off the floor through *cou de pied* as you spring upwards and sideways into the air.

Bend your supporting leg in towards your working leg, in a well turned-out position with your back foot still slightly behind your front foot.

Land into a *demi-plié* on your back foot, with your other leg just above *cou de pied*.

Close into fifth position (same foot in front as before) as you straighten your supporting leg.

Assemblés

This is a type of jump that starts from one foot, but lands on both. It can be done in different directions and can also be done with a change of feet 'over' and 'under'.

For an *assemblé derrière*, begin in fifth *demi-plié* with your back foot *sur le cou de pied*.

Use your *battement frappé* to strike through the floor, stretching your leg out to second and lifting you into the air. (Don't swing the leg. Make sure you stretch it strongly and precisely.)

Stretch your supporting leg underneath you as you lift up and travel.

Just before you land, bring both legs together (same foot in front), then lower into a *demi plié*.

Sissonnes

There are several different types of *sissonne*, including small neat jumps and large flying leaps. All start from two feet but some *sissones* end with one leg held up in the air (*sissonne fondue*). In others you close the leg quickly after landing (*sissonne fermê*).

First practise a *sissonne simple*. Beginning in a *demi-plié* in fifth, spring up into the air drawing your legs together (keep the same leg in front).

Land on one leg in a *demi-plié* (either the front or the back leg), holding the other *sur le cou de pied* (either *derrière* or *devant*).

Move on to a *sissonne fermé*, which travels across the floor as well as upwards. You should feel as if you're flying when you dance this step and try to express this lift and lightness with your body. *Sissonnes fermés* can be performed *en avant* (forwards), *en arrière* (backwards), or *à la seconde* (sideways).

To perform a *sissonne fermé en avant*, start with your legs in fifth *demi-plié*.

Leap up into the air, stretching the legs into an *arabesque* line.

Land on your front leg and sink into a *demi-plié*, while holding your stretched back leg in an *arabesque* line behind you. Try not to let this lifted leg dip as you land.

Quickly and smoothly continue the movement by closing your back leg to fifth through *battement tendu*.

Perfection Pointers

Changements

As your *changements* get stronger, you'll be able to beat your legs in front and behind each other in the air while still keeping them absolutely stretched and pointed. In an *entrechat quatre*, you cross your legs twice: begin in fifth position, leap into the air drawing your legs up but immediately taking the front leg to the back, return your front leg while still up in the air with your legs stretched, and then land back in fifth. As you jump higher you'll be able to add in more beats – a dancer called Wayne Sleep could do an *entrechat douze*: crossing the legs five times! You'll also learn how to add beats into other types of jump too.

Échappés sautés

Once you've mastered jumping from fifth to second, try jumping from fifth to fourth position. You can also then practise a *grand échapé*, where you jump higher, drawing your legs together in the air and only opening them out to the new position at the last minute. The lower you bend the higher you should jump – but take care not to exagerate your *plié*. Try to remember to land as lightly as possible and avoid any crash landings!

Assemblés

Assemblés are often performed as a big leap, with leg beats added in before landing. They can also be turned in the air.

Sissonnes

Like *assemblés*, larger *sissonnes* can also be beaten or turned, to make very exciting, dramatic movements.

Ballon

Ballon literally means 'bounce', and when you are an advanced student you will try to link jumping steps together so that you look as if you are lightly springing and bouncing across the stage.

A *ballotté* is a particularly springy step which bounces from one foot to the other, rocking backwards and forwards. It takes a lot of balance and strength to stop you from tilting over.

A *ballonné* is another especially bouncy step, which involves springing up and landing on the same one foot. This takes lots of strength and good use of your *demi-plié*.

97

SPOTLIGHTS

Improving your **ballon** *will help you make large leaps in which you look as though you are hanging in the air for an instant at the highest point of the jump. The legendary Nijinsky was so amazing at leaping off the stage into the wings without losing any height that he left his audiences spellbound, wondering whether he really could fly!*

Jetés

A jump which takes off from one leg and lands on the other is called a *jeté*. A *grand jeté* is a huge leap where the dancer seems to soar through the air, performing *grands battements* with both legs into the splits position. Different *arabesque* lines are shown through the body and arms.

With even more work you might one day be able to perform a *flick jeté*, where the angle of the *grand jeté* is tilted and the upper body thrown backwards at the same time. This movement is both athletic and expressive at the same time.

Beaten leaps

It will take years of practice before you can leap high enough through the air to beat your legs together and open them up (as in grand battement) before you land, while at the same time making a beautiful curved line through your body and along your arms. *Cabrioles* and *brisés volés* are extremely hard to perform, but lead dancers make them look effortless. Some testing roles, such as the Bluebird variation in *The Sleeping Beauty*, link together sequences of these arching, beating, high-springing steps with outstretched *port de bras*, so the dancer really does look as if they are flying.

Tours en l'air

Many *grand allegro* jumps for boys involve turning in the air – often while travelling around the stage at the same time. A *tour en l'air* is a spectacular turning jump that stays on the spot.

Starting from a *demi-plié* in fifth, with your arms in third (same arm as leg in front of you), spring up into the air drawing the legs together and bringing your outstretched arm into first. (Be sure not to start to turn before your body and legs are straight and pulled up in the air.) Use your spotting technique to turn a full circle *en dehors*, bringing your back leg to the front, and landing in a smooth fifth *demi-plié*.

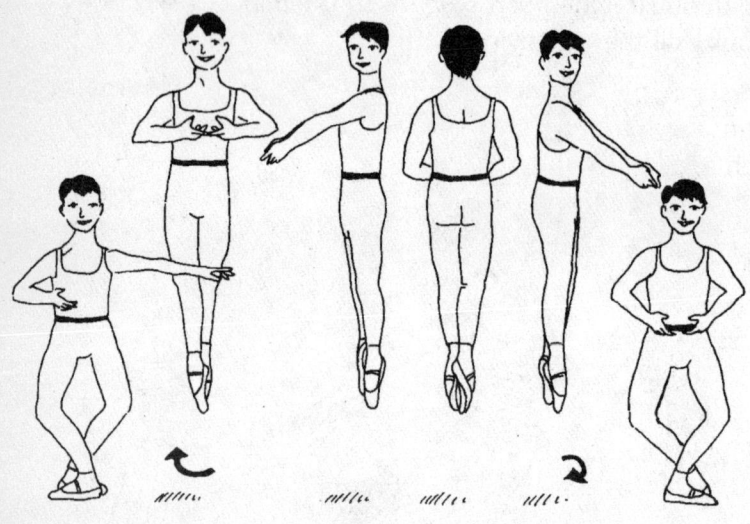

Some male principal dancers manage to perform double or triple t*ours en l'air* and land without a wobble in a dramatic pose on one knee. Spectacular!

Developing technique

As if *port de bras*, *adage* and *allegro* aren't enough to master, there are other specialist techniques you will need to get to grips with if you want to be a good ballet dancer. And not all of them involve just your physical ability!

If I can't talk, how do I say what I mean?

Dancers don't use words to say what they mean. Instead they rely on their bodies and faces to talk to their audience, with their make-up, costume and scenery all helping to tell the story or give clues to their ideas and feelings.

Years ago, many choreographers began to use the same acting gestures, so certain poses took on set meanings, such as:

fear   ask or beg   sleep   death

Developing technique

These easily recognisable movements became the silent language of classical ballet, a type of sign language that you can learn to understand just like reading words.

When you mime:

- Hold yourself and move with the same technique that you use in the rest of your ballet dancing.
- Always look turned-out, controlled and graceful, no matter what ideas or feelings you are trying to get across.
- Use your imagination so you really feel like the character you are trying to portray.
- Don't exaggerate your movements, although they should be large and clear enough for the audience to see.
- Try to express yourself with sincerity, rather than just 'play-acting'.

STAR PROFILE

LYNN SEYMOUR

Lynn Seymour was born in 1939 in Canada. She trained in Vancouver before coming to England to study at the Sadler's Wells Ballet School (now the Royal Ballet School). Lynn rose rapidly to the rank of ballerina and it was her wonderful acting ability that made her such a special dancer, excelling in demanding dramatic roles such as the leads in the tragedies *Romeo and Juliet* and *Manon*. She worked many times with choreographer Kenneth MacMillan to create new roles, also performing with contemporary dance companies and becoming a distinguished teacher and artistic director. Even though Lynn Seymour is now nearly 60 years old, you can still see her perform today in character roles (which involve more acting than dancing).

What is character dancing?

Character dancing does not primarily mean acting out a character, such as a witch or fairy, a prince or princess, a skater or a schoolgirl. Each different country of the world has its own type of traditional dancing – often very different to ballet – which reflects the character of its people. Russian folk dancers stamp their feet and hold their heads and arms proudly, performing leg kicks, deep knee bends and high jumps. The traditional dancing of Spain is the fiery drumming of the flamenco. Dancing from Thailand is elegantly slow and gliding, involving thoughtful and balanced a-symmetrical poses.

Russia

Spain

Thailand

Developing technique

Choreographers have always liked to introduce dance styles from other countries into their work to contrast with the ballet dancing, adding a change of pace, mood and colour. For instance, *Coppélia* includes a swirling Polish mazurka, a joyful Spanish fan dance, and a lively Scottish reel. It's great fun to try these traditional types of dance, and you'll find that the suppleness, strength and jumping ability you're developing through your ballet training will help you perform these folk dances well. Think about whether the spirit of the country is proud, passionate, joyful, sad or quiet, and dance the steps in this way.

Character shoes

You may wear a special type of shoe for character dancing. These have a small heel and look much more like everyday shoes than ballet shoes, although they have a special non-slip leather sole. Girls' character shoes usually fasten with a strap that buttons across, while boys' are usually lace-up. Certain eastern European dances are performed wearing character boots.

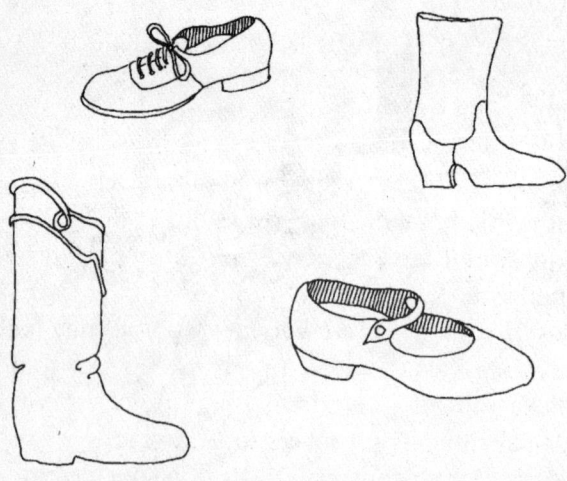

When can I dance on my toes?

You should always wait to try dancing on *pointe* until your teacher tells you that you're ready. No matter how good you are at ballet or how hard you have worked, this won't be until you're at least 11 years old because you can damage the still-growing bones in your feet if you try to make them bear all your body-weight before they are properly developed.

Buying your first pair of *pointe* shoes is very exciting. It's a sign that you've made good progress with your dancing and have developed strength in your legs and feet. But although you're entitled to feel very proud of your determined training so far, buying your first pair of *pointe* shoes marks the start of even more hard work!

- Remember that *pointe* shoes are all very different, and it's not as simple as just choosing a pair in your everyday shoe size.
- Always buy your *pointe* shoes from a specialist shop where trained staff will fit the right pair for your feet.
- Even the right pair of *pointe* shoes may still be quite uncomfortable to dance in for a while!
- Although *pointe* shoes are often called 'blocked' shoes, there aren't in fact 'blocks' in them at all. The toes are made of layers of satin, paper, a material called burlap, and glue, which makes them very hard and stiff.
- You might find it hard to bend your foot enough to rise up properly on *demi-pointe*.
- The soles of your shoes are very thick – you may feel as though you're balancing on a narrow ledge, or that you don't make your usual arch when you point your foot. (This specially thickened sole is to support the underneath of your foot while you're balancing on your toes.)

Developing technique

- Your *pointe* shoes *will* soften up as you use them. However, until they do, you might want to put a little animal wool inside your 'blocks' to cushion your feet against the hard ends.

- Some dancers harden the skin on their toes by rubbing in surgical spirit every night, so they're less inclined to blister and rub!

- Many dancers also flex their shoes in their hands (or even bash their shoes on the floor) to soften up the sole. However, despite all these things, nothing will ultimately make your shoes mould comfortably round your feet unless you wear them and dance in them. This means that, unfortunately, many dancers have sore feet all the time because of continually having to 'break in' new *pointe* shoes. Lucky boys, of course, don't have to go through the agonies of dancing on *pointe*!

The length of time it takes for a pair of *pointe* shoes to wear out depends not only on how much you use them but also on what types of roles you dance. Former principal dancer Karen Smith says that when dancing the lead role of Odette/Odile in *Swan Lake*, her left shoes used to get worn down much faster than her right shoes, as many of the steps 'led' with the left! Professional dancers use both old and new *pointe* shoes to perform in. (They sometimes darn the toes of new *pointe* shoes to make the satin last longer.) Brand new *pointe* shoes are good for partnerwork, as they give you a really hard base for balancing on one leg or spinning on your toes. Older, more flexible shoes are better for scenes involving fast, neat footwork, as your feet can move in them more easily and the softer toes don't make so much noise on the floor when you run or jump.

Relevés at the *barre* are the best way to learn how to rise up on *pointe*. Begin facing the *barre* before trying them side-on, and practise them in each position of the feet:

To perform a *relevé* in first, begin with a *demi-plié* in first position.

Smoothly pull up your legs tightly, being sure to peel all of your foot off the floor bit by bit as you rise up on to your toes. (You mustn't 'jump up' on to your toes and miss out going through *demi-pointe*). Keep your tummy muscles tight and your body lifted, and try to find your centre of balance – which may be a little further forward than you think it should be. Be careful to hold your turnout well and your feet straight and stretched.

Smoothly lower back through *demi-pointe* into your *demi-plié*, in a controlled movement.

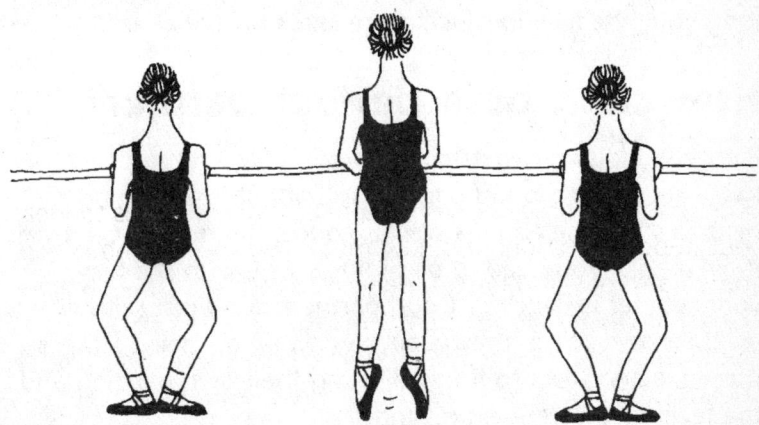

Developing technique

Next try *échappés* at the *barre*, firstly facing the *barre* and from fifth to second position and back to fifth, then sideways on to the *barre* and from fifth to fourth position and returning to fifth:

Begin with a *demi-plié* and spring into your next position on *pointe* by using all the muscles in your feet to push upwards and along the floor.

Return back to your starting *demi-plié* by feeling your whole foot lower bit by bit through the floor.

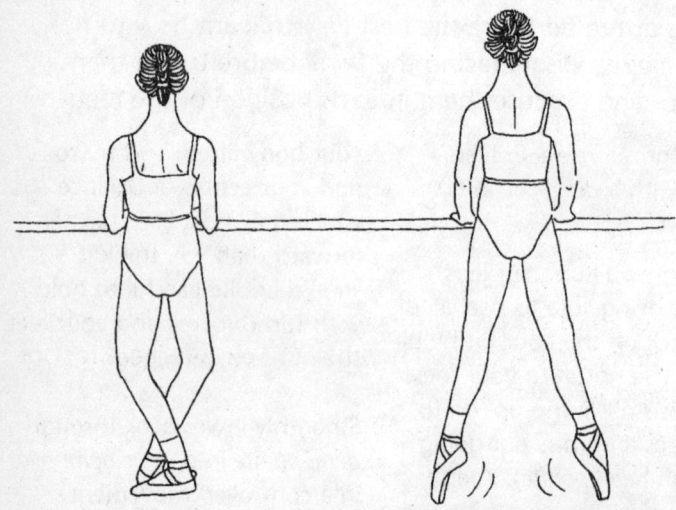

Keep persevering with your pointework practice and before long you'll be feeling much more like a ballerina!

How can I be a perfect partner?

Partnerwork is known as *pas de deux* – literally 'steps for two'. But being a good partner isn't about just dancing next to someone else. As well as concentrating on your own movements, you need to be highly sensitive to the way your partner is dancing. Good partners don't just selfishly do their own thing; they're acutely aware of their partner's presence and react to it by adjusting their own dancing and the feelings they are expressing.

Your first experience of *pas de deux* will be through *supported adage*, where the boy and girl work close together without lifting. Everyone feels uncomfortable about moving very close to someone for the first time, but after you've got over the initial embarrassment of touching a person you don't know well, partners often become good friends and have a lot of fun dancing together.

Pas de deux work allows dancers to achieve more than they can on their own. For instance, the way the boy is supporting the girl in this variation of third *arabesque*, and complementing her with his own body shape, gives a much more expressive effect of longing and yearning than if the girl were dancing an *arabesque* alone. She can also stand on *pointe* for longer than she could without support.

Developing technique

In the same way, a supported pirouette allows a girl to make more turns than she would do unaided. If she moves off balance, it's up to her partner to correct her without the mistake being noticed.

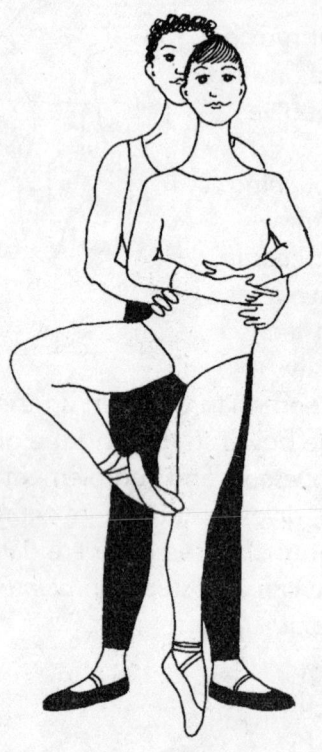

The supported balances, straight lifts, and travelling lifts of *pas de deux* work require a lot of trust between partners. It can be very dangerous to try movements such as a supported fall or a swallow lift if you perform them half-heartedly, as you'll be making your partner strain and work extra hard to make up for your lack of effort. This can cause serious injuries. All *pas de deux* work requires precise timing, co-ordination, and strength on the part of both the boy and girl.

Swallow lift

Supported fall

SPOTLIGHTS

THE MOST FAMOUS BALLET PARTNERSHIP

Margot Fonteyn was already established as a renowned ballerina with the Royal Ballet when an extremely talented dancer called Rudolph Nureyev arrived from Russia in 1961. Nureyev was young – only 23 years old – and full of enthusiasm and originality. At the time, the main role of the male principal was to support the ballerina and 'show her off', but Nureyev had other ideas. With his amazing technique and creativity he showed people that the principal male role could (and should) be at least as important as the ballerina's – which was revolutionary in ballet at the time! Nureyev and Fonteyn developed a truly magical dancing relationship: as two of the greatest ever dancers in their own right, they complemented each other's dancing in a way that no other partner could do. At their debut performance together in Giselle *at London's Covent Garden in 1962, they took 23 curtain calls – the start of a legendary partnership.*

9 Making a ballet

Dancers spend years of hard work training for the chance to join a company and perform in different ballets. And each company has its own unique approach to the type of ballets they present. All dancers have their own strengths and weaknesses, but they must be versatile enough to turn their abilities and technique to some very different kinds of work.

Who decides which ballets a company will perform?

The artistic director. He or she will select ballets from well-known favourites like *Coppélia*, *Cinderella* and *Giselle* and commission people to create exciting (and riskier!) new ballets.

Where is everybody?

Making a ballet

Sometimes an artistic director will decide to present a 'triple bill' of three pieces of work often combining old and new choreography. The different ballets a company can stage are known as its *repertoire*.

How is a choreographer chosen for a new ballet?

Some companies have their own special choreographer. In others, an artistic director makes sure that she or he watches a wide range of other company's work in order to spot choreographers who have exciting new ideas. When the artistic director is told of an interesting new choreographer, she or he will ask them to send a video of their work before possibly inviting them to discuss their ideas. Once a choreographer has been issued with a contract to create a new ballet for the company they are said to have been commissioned.

Who makes up the music for a new ballet?

Sometimes a choreographer is inspired to create a new ballet by music that already exists. For instance, Maurice Béjart has created a ballet for his company that mixes the music of the rock group Queen with that of Mozart. However, a composer will often be commissioned to make up special music for a new ballet in much the same way as a choreographer. The two will work closely together, discussing their thoughts and feelings with the artistic director, to create a type of music that fits the dancing in the right way. Before the composer arrives at the final score (music), they will have tried and discarded many different approaches.

SPOTLIGHTS

Before the 19th Century, ballets were danced to music that was enjoyable to listen to but which didn't really complement the steps. It was a French composer, Adolphe Adam (1803-1856) who made a breakthrough in ballet music when, for Giselle, he used the musical idea of leitmotifs. The main characters each have their own individual tunes which repeat and change as the ballet unfolds and the character develops. In this way, the music itself creates drama, heightening the effects being portrayed by the dancers. If you listen to Prokofiev's musical score for Romeo and Juliet, you'll easily feel how leitmotifs can help dancers to create their characters.

How does a choreographer make up the steps?

Before starting to make up the steps for a new ballet, the choreographer will have worked out a storyline, exploring the characters and the action, and doing any research into the subject if necessary. If the new work is to be a theme ballet, the choreographer will have thought through his or her feelings and ideas about the subject very thoroughly. All this background work will have given them ideas about the kind of movements they want the dancers to make.

Um.... Maybe that move's not such a good idea after all.

Some choreographers will then go on to work out most of the steps before they start rehearsing with the dancers. Others will wait until they have the dancers in front of them in the studio to decide on the steps. Sometimes, positions the choreographer has imagined will not work out in reality. In other cases, watching the dancers' bodies move suggests possibilities – or the dancers themselves will often have their own ideas. A choreographer may also create a role especially for a particular dancer and their best qualities.

How do the choreographer and the dancers remember the steps?

With so many ideas floating around and different steps being tried out, remembering what was agreed at rehearsal can be confusing! Ballets used to be remembered and passed on to others by the people who created and danced them. So any steps which were forgotten were lost forever. But today, a specially-trained dance notator can write everything down accurately using a type of code. They record what each dancer is doing with every bit of their body at each count of the music. They then make a combined record which shows the movements of all the dancers together called a score. There are two main types of notation: Benesh notation and Labanotation.

How long does it take to create a new ballet from start to finish?

Preparation for elements of the production such as the making of the costumes and scenery, will probably begin weeks or even months before the dancers start rehearsing the ballet. The actual rehearsals for a new ballet will start between 5 to 10 weeks from the planned date of its first performance. You may be surprised by how quick this seems! But the more time a company takes to develop a new ballet, the less time there is available to rehearse and perform its existing repertoire. Fewer performances means less money coming in from ticket sales, which will put the future of the company in jeopardy.

Dancers therefore need the intelligence to learn and remember new ballets very quickly. Their training will equip them with the discipline needed to practise and perfect them in a short space of time. They are used to a choreographer making changes right up to the last minute before the ballet's first night – or even changing things later on, after seeing the ballet performed properly in front of an audience. Creating a ballet involves many people, who all need to work together as part of a large team to make it a success.

 # A ballet dancer's life

Ask any ballet dancer how they feel about their life and they'll say that they love it, they wouldn't do anything else – but that it's desperately hard! If you want to be a professional ballet dancer (and there are many other reasons to enjoy learning ballet), there are lots of things you should consider before setting your heart on a path that's filled with possible frustration and heartbreak as well as immense satisfaction and fun!

Is it true that if you work really hard, you'll make it to the top?

Sadly, this isn't necessarily the case. Ballet makes tough demands on you physically and, although you may be determined, you must also be realistic. People's bodies aren't all made the same. No matter how many hours of practise you put in, if your hips are too tight, your back is inflexible, if you grow too tall or not tall enough, you will never be a professional dancer. But if you really love dancing, don't be put off by things you cannot change. Why not think about training to be a teacher rather than a performer? Or develop your dramatic skills with acting classes. Or use the technique and abilities you are learning in your ballet to enjoy lessons in other forms of dance such as tap or jazz.

Can you be too fat to dance?

Take no notice if someone tells you that you're too fat to dance. It's true that professional ballet dancers can't have any awkward lumps or bumps, but as you grow up your body goes through all sorts of strange changes – including phases where usually slim people put on weight. Harold King, Artistic Director of the City Ballet of London, advises young dancers not to get despondent and give up because of their weight as it will eventually settle down in the end. So eat healthily to make sure your body is fit enough for strenuous ballet classes and stick with it!

Do you have to go to residential ballet school to become a professional ballet dancer?

It's not impossible to become a professional without going to a residential school, if you have an excellent teacher and you work very hard indeed. But going to a residential school will give you the best chance of getting all the direction and support you need to succeed in your training. You can audition for a residential school when you are 11. At the audition they will look carefully to see if you have the correct physique for ballet. As well as checking for things like strong, arched feet and that your joints are neither too loose or too stiff, they may also want to know the height of close adult relatives, from which they can have an indication of whether you will grow to be finally too small or too tall. Having the right type of body for ballet is even more important at this stage than your dancing ability. If you are accepted by a school, you will have regular dancing assessments and, if your teachers don't think you're making enough progress or if your body is developing the wrong way, you may be asked to leave.

A ballet dancer's life

You can try again for a full-time ballet school, such as the Royal Ballet Upper School, when you are 15 or 16. Lessons at a senior school include repertory, hair, and make-up lessons as well as intensive ballet training, as the time is looming frighteningly close when you will need to find a job!

How do you get into a ballet company?

The artistic director of a ballet company is in charge of hiring – and firing! – dancers. If you are at a residential ballet school, you will audition for the company attached to your school when their artistic director comes to watch one of your classes. If you are not at such a school, you will need to go to an 'open' audition where you are watched by the artistic director in a ballet class taken by one of the company's own teachers. These auditions are advertised on the noticeboards at major professional dance studios and in professional magazines and newspapers.

An audition is a pretty ruthless selection procedure. There may be hundreds of dancers competing for only two or three places in the company and if you are not feeling well or make mistakes out of nervousness, you may not get a second chance to show what you can do.

What happens if you are not accepted into a company?

Competition for ballet companies is so fierce that it's important to learn as many other skills as possible to broaden your availability for work. For instance, ballet dancers with excellent singing ability can audition for musicals like *The Phantom of the Opera*. Opera companies sometimes need classically-trained dancers for their productions. Dancers who can act or do jazz and tap can also get the chance to try for parts in pop videos and television shows.

What happens if you are accepted into a company?

A ballet company has a clear structure of rankings and you would start at the bottom in the *corps de ballet*. *Coryphées* are exceptional members of the *corps de ballet* who are occasionally given solo parts. *Soloists* perform on their own, and may also understudy principal roles so they can take over if the principal is ill or injured. *Principals* dance the most exciting roles in ballets and may guest star with other companies throughout the world.

How long will a ballet career last?

Because ballet is so physically demanding most professional dancers just get too tired to carry on with their career beyond the age of 30 or 35. Only a few dancers are able to continue beyond this age with a career that enables them to perform on stage.

Even if you're absolutely sure that all you'll want to do for the rest of your life is ballet, unexpected things can cut short your career.

A ballet dancer's life

Karen Smith had a highly successful career that began at the Royal Ballet School, before dancing all over the world. She was particularly good at *soubrette* roles (those involving showy fast spins and jumps) and rose to the rank of principal, dancing the lead in all the major ballets. In one blow, Karen's career was destroyed when she broke her neck in a car crash. For three months she was paralysed and wondered whether she would walk again, let alone dance. Since then, Karen has rebuilt her wasted muscles and learned more about her body as she recovered, retraining as a practitioner of physical therapies such as massage and Pilates technique. She misses performing, but very much enjoys coaching professionals and teaching adults who learn ballet simply for the joy of it!

Dancer and actress Julia Lintott always wanted to do ballet more than anything else. However, after she'd completed her training she was shocked to find that ballet wasn't really what she wanted after all. Julia felt that she wanted to express herself in ways that weren't allowed by ballet's strict rules. Leaving classical training behind, she went first to Italy to study mime, and has since had an enjoyable career as both a commercial dancer and actress in theatre productions from musicals to the Royal Shakespeare Company. She still loves ballet very much, but is glad that she didn't choose the strict lifestyle of a professional ballet dancer.

Whether or not dancing becomes your career, ballet can play an important part in your life, and give you lots of enjoyment now and in the future. Good luck!

Want to know more?

Useful addresses • Websites

The following organisations can help you to find a ballet class near you:

British Association of Teachers of Dancing
23 Marywood Square
Glasgow G41 2BP
Tel 0141 423 4029

*Cecchetti Society
(Classical Ballet)*
Imperial House
22-26 Paul Street
London EC2A 4QE
Tel 0171 377 1577
also
302 High Street
Northcote VIC 3770
Australia
Tel (03) 9482 2733

Council for Dance Education and Training (UK)
Riverside Studios
Crisp Road
London W6 9RL
Tel 0181 741 5084

Imperial Society of Teachers of Dancing
Imperial House
22-26 Paul Street
London EC2A 4QE
Tel 0171 377 1577

International Dance Teachers' Association
International House
76 Bennett Road
Brighton BN2 5JL
Tel 01273 685652

Royal Academy of Dancing
36 Battersea Square
London SW11 3RA
Tel 0171 223 0091
also
20 Farrell Avenue
Darlinghurst NSW 2010
Australia
Tel (02) 9331 4111

Want to know more?

You can find out more about the international ballet scene on these websites:

CyberDance – Ballet on the Net
http://www.thepoint.net/~raw/dance.htm
A collection of over 2000 links to classical ballet and modern dance resources on the Net.

The Ballet Modern FAQ
http://www.panix.com/~twp/dance/faq_1.htm
Answers to frequently asked questions about ballet.

English National Ballet
http://www.ballet.org.uk/
Highlights of the season, guest artists and some excellent photographs.

Royal Ballet School
http://www.hubcom.com/rbs/
A history of the school along with information about how to apply and auditions.

The Australian Ballet
http://www.vicnet.net.au/vicnet/ballet/ballet.html
Data on the company, its forthcoming performances and its education programme.

New York City Ballet
http://www.nycballet.com/
Including trivia, puzzles and a photo gallery.

The Bolshoi Theatre, Ballet and Opera
http://www.alincom/com/bolshoi/index.htm
A history of this famous company plus details of classic and modern performances.

Glossary

(A rough guide to the pronunciation of the French terms is given in italics.)

abstract ballets ballets which have no story or theme but which display the dancers' technical skills

adage (*adarj*) steps and movements which flow in a slow, controlled way

à la seconde (*alla secondh*) second position

alignment lining up parts of your body to make flowing, elegant, unbroken lines

allegro (*aleg-row*) fast, lively movements

allongé (*alonj-ay*) a hand position in which the palms are turned down and the fingers extended

arabesque (*arra-besk*) a ballet pose in which you balance on one leg with the other leg stretched out behind you, making a beautiful line from your fingertips down to your toes

assemblé (*assom-blay*) a jump which springs from two feet and lands on two feet

à terre (*ah tair*) on the ground

attitude a ballet pose in which you balance on one leg with the other leg bent either behind or in front

backcloth or backdrop the large piece of material or scenery at the back of the stage which is painted to depict the scene or theme

ballet blanc (*ballay blonk*) 'white ballet' – any ballet or scenes in which the female dancers all wear long, Romantic-style ballet dresses

ballon (*bal-on*) the ability to bounce and spring

battement frappé (*bat-mon frap-ay*) an exercise in which you stand on one leg and strike the floor with the other

battement tendu (*bat-mon ton-dew*) an exercise in which you stretch one leg from one of the five positions into an open pointed position and then draw it back

batterie (*bat-er-ree*) jumps in which the legs beat across each other

bourrée (*boor-ay*) a step involving light, rapid and precise footwork

bras (*bra*) arms

bras bas (*bra bah*) holding the arms in a low position

centre of balance when, in any position, perfectly balanced

changement (*shonj-mon*) a jump which begins from third or fifth and ends with the other foot in front

character dancing traditional dancing from different countries

character role a role which requires a lot of acting

choreographer someone who creates ballets or dances

choreography the steps of a ballet

choreologist someone who uses notation systems to record dances

choreology the recording of dance movements, using special notation systems

corps de ballet (*cor duh bal-ay*) dancers who perform together in a large group

Glossary

croisé (cwoz-ay) turning the body slightly to the corner with the leg nearest the audience in front, so the position looks 'crossed' to the audience

degagé (dega-jay) a position where a dancer stands on one leg and points the other to touch the floor in any direction around her

demi-plié (demee-pleeay) a half knee-bend in one of the five positions of the feet

demi-pointe (demee-point) on the balls of the feet

derriére (derry-air) behind

dessous (duh-sues) under (when the working foot passes behind the supporting foot)

desus (duh-sue) over (when the working foot passes in front of the supporting foot)

devant (duh-von) in front

développé (dev-lopay) an exercise in which the leg is slowly unfolded in the air into an extended, open position

divertissement (de-vertiss-mon) a short dance which shows off a dancer's skills rather than progresses a story, or which contrasts with the style of other dances for variety and entertainment

ecarté (ay-car-teh) positioning the body on a diagonal with one leg in second, so the position looks opened out and 'flat'

echappée (ay-shap-ay) a movement in which both legs move apart into an open position

effacé (ay-fas-ay) turning the body slightly to the corner with the leg furthest away from the audience

in front, so the position looks 'open'

en avant (ona-von) travelling forwards

en croix (on cwah) where the working leg moves in front, to the side and behind, making the shape of a cross

en dedans (on duhdons) inwardly (or towards the supporting leg)

en dehors (on day-or) outwardly (or away from the supporting leg)

en face (on fas) facing squarely towards the audience

en l'air (on lair) in the air

en pointe (on point) dancing on the tips of the toes

en tournant (on tour-non) turning

enchainement (on-shayn-mon) a series of steps linked together

entrechat (ontra-sha) a jump in which the legs are beaten in the air one or more times

extension a dancer's ability to extend one leg high into the air

fermé (fare-may) when the feet are in a closed position

fondu (fon-dew) a flowing, melting movement

fouettés (fwet-ay) a spin on one leg in which the working leg whips in and out during each turn

frappé (frap-ay) a rapid striking movement

glissade (glee-sarde) a travelling step that glides across the floor

grand (grond) large or big

grand battement (grond bat-mon) sweeping leg kicks

grand jeté (grond jet-ay) a leap through the air with the legs outstretched

grand plié (grond plee-ay) a full knee-bend in the five positions

jambe (jom) leg
jeté (jet-ay) a jump which takes off from one leg and lands on one leg

Labanotation a coded system, devised in the 1920s by Rodulf von Laban, used to record dances
leitmotif (light moteef) a phrase in ballet music which represents a character
line the graceful, flowing outline a dancer makes with her body

ouvert (oo-vairt) an open foot position

pas couru (par coor-ew) run
pas de chat (par de shah) literally 'step of the cat' – a travelling jump
pas de deux (par duh der) a dance where a boy partners a girl
penchée (pon-shay) leaning or tilted
petit (puh-tee) small
petit battement (puh-tee bat mon) small beating movements in front and behind
pied (peeay) foot
pirouette (pir-oo-et) a spin on one leg
placing holding each part of the body with correct technique
port de bras (poor duh bra) arm movements through the five positions

relevé (rel-ev-ay) an exercise in which you rise up on the balls of your feet and then lower again
répétituer (rep-et-e-tur) a person who leads ballet rehearsals
repertoire (rep-er-twah) the ballets that a company has prepared and is equipped to perform
retiré (ret-ear-ray) a position in which the toes of the working leg are lifted just below the knee of the supporting leg

révérence (rev-er-onse) a special type of ballet bow
rolling of the feet incorrect technique where the feet roll inwards from the ankle (often caused by trying too hard to achieve perfect turnout)
ronde de jambe (ron duh jam) an exercise in which one leg marks out a semi-circle

sauter (sew-tair) to jump
score the music for a ballet
set the scenery and props
sickling pointing your foot incorrectly
sissone (see-sone) a jump from two feet to one foot
soutenu (soo-ten-ue) sustained
spotting a technique to stop dancers getting dizzy when they turn
supported adage where a boy partners a girl closely without lifting her
sur (soor) on or upon
sur le cou de pied (soor le coo de peeay) a position in which the working foot rests on or around the supporting ankle
syllabus (sil-a-bus) the range of movements a ballet organisation requires you to study and perform for examinations

technique (teck-neeke) the 'rules' of classical ballet style
tendu (ton-do) stretched
theme ballets ballets which do not have a story but which explore ideas, feelings or moods
tour en l'air (tour on lair) a turn in the air
turnout holding the legs in a position rotated outwardly from the hip

Index